Another m...
pursuit car...

The hunters didn't give a damn about potential bystanders. Professionals. Nothing but victory or death would stop them.

Except, Bolan was determined they wouldn't win.

Which left one option.

He had to find a killing ground that minimized the prospect of collateral damage. There, he'd make a stand and see what came of it. If he could—

Suddenly another pair of headlights glared from behind the chase car.

Reinforcements maybe? If that were true, there could be anywhere from two to five, or even six guns in the second vehicle. The odds *against* survival might have just doubled.

But Bolan had beaten worse odds in the past and walked away. Even if death was certain for himself, he would fight until his last round had been fired, then take it hand to hand.

The hunting party's scarred survivors would not soon forget their meeting with the Executioner.

MACK BOLAN ®
The Executioner

The Executioner

Don Pendleton's

SURVIVAL MISSION

A GOLD EAGLE BOOK FROM

W🌐RLDWIDE®

TORONTO • NEW YORK • LONDON
AMSTERDAM • PARIS • SYDNEY • HAMBURG
STOCKHOLM • ATHENS • TOKYO • MILAN
MADRID • WARSAW • BUDAPEST • AUCKLAND

For Specialist Salvatore Augustine Giunta
"Unwavering courage, selflessness and decisive leadership while under extreme enemy fire."
Korengal Valley, Afghanistan, 25 October 2007

First edition September 2012

ISBN-13: 978-0-373-64406-3

Special thanks and acknowledgment to
Michael Newton for his contribution to this work.

Recycling programs for this product may not exist in your area.

SURVIVAL MISSION

Printed in U.S.A.

And whoso shall receive one such little child in my name receiveth me. But whoso shall offend one of these little ones which believe in me, it were better for him that a millstone were hanged about his neck, and that he were drowned in the depth of the sea.

—Matthew 18:5–6

Forget about millstones. This time, the cleansing fire.

—Mack Bolan

THE
MACK BOLAN
LEGEND

Nothing less than a war could have fashioned the destiny of the man called Mack Bolan. Bolan earned the Executioner title in the jungle hell of Vietnam.

But this soldier also wore another name—Sergeant Mercy. He was so tagged because of the compassion he showed to wounded comrades-in-arms and Vietnamese civilians.

Mack Bolan's second tour of duty ended prematurely when he was given emergency leave to return home and bury his family, victims of the Mob. Then he declared a one-man war against the Mafia.

He confronted the Families head-on from coast to coast, and soon a hope of victory began to appear. But Bolan had broken society's every rule. That same society started gunning for this elusive warrior—to no avail.

So Bolan was offered amnesty to work within the system against terrorism. This time, as an employee of Uncle Sam, Bolan became Colonel John Phoenix. With a command center at Stony Man Farm in Virginia, he and his new allies—Able Team and Phoenix Force—waged relentless war on a new adversary: the KGB.

But when his one true love, April Rose, died at the hands of the Soviet terror machine, Bolan severed all ties with Establishment authority.

Now, after a lengthy lone-wolf struggle and much soul-searching, the Executioner has agreed to enter an "arm's-length" alliance with his government once more, reserving the right to pursue personal missions in his Everlasting War.

Prologue

The stranger was out of his element, running on animal rage and a vestige of hope that grew fainter with each hour's passage. He didn't know the city but could read a map. He didn't speak the country's foremost language but had drilled sufficiently in German and Russian as a younger man to get along. Locals would take him for a tourist if he didn't push his luck too far, come down on them too hard.

That was the rough part, trying to act casual when every instinct he possessed was telling him to run amok and burn the goddamned city down if that was what it took to reach his goal. How many lives was he prepared to sacrifice in the pursuit of one he still held precious?

Pick a number. Any number. Were there seven billion people on the planet yet?

The only one that mattered was beyond his grasp so far, but he was getting closer.

He could feel it, with the ache inside that marked her loss.

He didn't know if she was still alive, or what condition he would find her in, if she was. Had she been lost beyond all doubt, there would have been no reason for the marginal display of calm he somehow managed to project. Under those circumstances, he could have let his fury off its leash and slaughtered everyone he met, until he found the ones responsible.

And introduced them to a taste of living hell on earth.

But for the moment, he was still Joe Tourist, soaking up the sights, dropping an offhand question into conversation here and there. His face was not a memorable one; the mirror in his hotel room confirmed it. If he hit no panic buttons, sounded no alarms, he should be able to get closer.

Maybe even close enough.

The first real hurdle had been finding the specific tools he needed in a foreign city, but he'd managed. Anywhere you went, worldwide, the managers of seedy bars and brothels were the secretkeepers. Taxi drivers could direct you to the action for a fee, and once you wormed your way into the pulsing heart of decadence, debased yourself enough to rule out any thought that you might be an undercover cop, the only thing that mattered was the price tag.

Anyplace on earth, a man—or woman—with sufficient cash in hand could find the means of degradation or the weapons of destruction. Name your poison. If a twisted mind was able to conceive it, currency could make the nightmare real.

So he was armed, not necessarily as well as he'd have liked, but adequately. He could kill a small battalion if his luck held, and he clung to the advantage of surprise. They shouldn't know that he was hunting them, not yet, but in the real world nothing could be taken on blind faith.

The arms dealer, for instance, would have underworld connections. Absolutely, beyond doubt. If he was talkative, told someone of the hardware he'd furnished to a foreigner—more to the point, a westerner—the ripples might begin to spread. Nothing that would identify the hunter yet, but once suspicion had been raised, the creatures dwelling in the city's netherworld would be alert. Watching and listening, reporting back to someone at the center of the loathsome spiderweb.

It was the spider that he wanted. Maybe more than one. But he'd be satisfied to save the gnat they'd snared, if only he could rescue her unharmed.

But if he'd come too late, as he feared—if she had been defiled, or worse—the stranger reckoned that a life or two in recompense might not be satisfactory.

He'd have to wait and see, after he checked the address he'd obtained from a young woman of the streets. She hadn't been in-

sulted when he told her that seventeen or eighteen years placed
her beyond the pale of his desires. In her profession, he supposed that she had heard and seen it all. Of course, he had to
pay the normal hourly rate and more besides, but once the deal
was struck she had been happy to oblige.

Or simply bored and sending one more pervert on his way.
Whatever.

Motive didn't matter to the stranger. All that counted was
the end result.

The street was named for some war hero of a bygone century who would have been forgotten, otherwise. He didn't rate
a statue, but they'd loaned his name to seven seedy blocks that
boasted tattoo parlors, pawnshops, hot-sheet hotels and diners
whose special was ptomaine roulette.

He'd spotted the red door, confirmed its street number. No
sign on the filthy brick wall to explain what went on inside the
three-story building. But then, he supposed, if you had this address there was no explanation required.

He rang the bell, waited and kept his face deadpan as someone scrutinized him through a peephole. Thirty seconds later
the door opened to reveal a bullet-headed, no-neck slab of muscle in a pin-striped suit who glowered at the new arrival from
behind an often-broken nose.

"Kdo jste?" he inquired. *"Co chceš?"*

Tone dictates meaning, and the stranger on the stoop replied in German.

"Ich bekam diese Adresse finden sie ein Mädchen."

The man with the bullet-shaped head considered it, then
stood aside. He switched to German.

"Hereinkommen."

Stepping past him, waiting for the door to close, the stranger
timed his move, drawing his pistol, turning on his heel to swing
it as a bludgeon. But the target had already moved, a big fist
looping toward the gunman's face to strike him with explosive
force. He fell, half-conscious, clinging to the pistol for a moment, until more men suddenly surrounded him and wrenched
it from his grasp.

The man with the bullet-shaped head leaned close enough for drops of spittle to make impact as he spoke. English this time.

"You're one dumb bastard, eh? Who helps your little girlie now?"

1

Prague, Czech Republic

The Vltava River winds through Prague's heart like a bloated, indolent serpent, winding under eighteen bridges, gliding past squatting warehouses and spires of classic architecture, passing stately homes and tenements. At first glance it seems lazy, placid, but its name derives from the Old German phrase *wilt ahwa*—and it still claims lives and property from time to time, as when it overflowed its banks in August of 2002.

Mack Bolan watched a ferry pass beneath the Palackého Bridge, checking his watch, then turned away and crossed a nearby street on foot. Sparse traffic let him take his chances without blaring horns. Orange streetlights lit the bridge and avenue beyond, while side streets made do with old-fashioned lamps on the corners and whatever light spilled from windows or small neon signs.

It was a seedy neighborhood, not criminal per se, but savvy residents of Prague knew better than to walk its streets alone by night, if that could be avoided. Muggers and pickpockets were a problem in the Czech Republic's capital and largest city, but they didn't worry Bolan. If his size, attitude and the expression on his face did not dissuade such people, he was carrying an ALFA semiautomatic pistol—the Defender model, used by many Czech police and military officers—chambered in .40 S&W with a twelve-round magazine and one round in the chamber. Extra magazines were slotted into Bolan's pockets, and he also carried a collapsible baton that added twenty inches to his normal reach.

His destination was a boxing gym called Oskar's, situated half a block west of the the Palackého Bridge. He wasn't looking for a sparring partner, and in fact was hoping that the place might already be closed. Civilians made things awkward and potentially disastrous, a fact his very presence in the city verified.

It was a rescue mission, plain but not so simple, since it currently involved two captives in distress, presumably confined at different locations. That is, if both were still alive.

The whole trip might turn out to be a waste of time, for all its planning and the hours that he'd spent in transit. If he reached the scene too late, there'd be no happy ending. Only payback, which was one of Bolan's specialties. Failing to save the day, he could at least do everything within his power to make sure the predators responsible did not survive to go on and commit such horrors again.

Time was not on Bolan's side. Before he'd even taken off from the United States, one of the prisoners he sought to liberate had already spent two days in hostile custody. The other had been gone for nine days, and he didn't want to think about what might have happened to her in that time.

He didn't want to, but the thoughts were unavoidable.

The ideal outcome of his mission would be the extraction of two living, healthy captives from whatever hell they'd been consigned to by their kidnappers. Bolan would settle for the *living* part, and cherished no illusions that the pair he'd come to find were being pampered by their captors as the days and nights went by. Whatever he found waiting for him at the end of his grim journey, Bolan understood that he was not responsible for healing. Saving lives—or ending them—was all that he aspired to on this night in Prague.

Business as usual.

Employing Bolan was a last resort for any situation. He was only called when every other means had failed and time was absolutely of the essence. And planning could only reach so far in the situations he found himself dealing with. The rest came down to raw audacity and ruthlessness.

He was the cleanup man.

The Executioner.

On this night, in Prague, he still had hope, but it was frail. He harbored no illusions about what might lie in store for him at Oskar's gym, or wherever the journey took him after that. He felt a sense of urgency, restrained by long experience, and had already steeled himself against the worst possible news.

Which wasn't death. Not even close.

Bolan had seen the worst—or some of it, at least—and it was always with him. Humans found more ways to torment one another than a sane mind could imagine, but the minds he dealt with on a daily basis only qualified as sane within a narrow legal definition. If a predator knew right from wrong and went ahead regardless, having the capacity to curb his cruelty, he was considered "sane."

Bolan didn't care.

The best way he had found to treat a brain seething with malice and contempt for all humanity was with a quick point-blank lobotomy.

Patients were waiting for him in the dark heart of Prague.

And the doctor was in.

FOUR HOURS HAD ELAPSED since Bolan's touchdown at Prague Ruzyně International Airport, traveling from Paris on Czech Airlines for the last leg of his twelve-hour trip from D.C., counting time spent in various terminals. Before he left the States, he'd put a Volvo S80 on hold with Europcar in Prague and found it waiting for him on arrival, waiting for delivery to Matthew Cooper. That name appeared on Bolan's primary passport, Virginia driver's license and the fully paid-up Visa Platinum card that covered any damage to the car while he was using it. He traveled light, a simple carry-on to dodge the extra baggage fees most airlines charged these days, but Bolan also needed tools to do the job at hand.

His first priority, therefore—like that of many other visitors to Prague—was shopping.

Bolan came prepared with a short list of names for suppliers gleaned from Stony Man Farm. He never knew exactly who compiled the lists, nor did he care, as long as there was inventory standing by when Bolan needed it. The list, three names in all, came with specific passwords that should open doors for Bolan as required.

His first stop was a bust, the shop in question vacant, with a placard in the window that directed him to Zorka Geislerová Ltd., presumably some kind of rental agent. Moving on, he found the second vendor just about to lock up for the night, but Bolan's coded phrase—*ryba je červená,* translated as "the fish is red" for reasons that he didn't bother pondering—bought him the time required to make his purchases.

He went for one-stop shopping, stocking up on everything he thought that he might need to do the job in Prague. The ALFA pistol was an easy choice, dependable and widely circulated in the Czech Republic, guaranteeing that its ammunition would be readily available. Next up, he chose a Vz. 58V assault rifle chambered in 7.62×39 mm, a folding-stock version of the country's standard-issue infantry weapon. It resembled the venerable AK-47, but internally it operated on a short-stroke gas piston the Czechs had designed for themselves, providing a cyclic rate of eight hundred rounds per minute and a maximum effective range exceeding four hundred yards, depending on the sights available.

In practice, though, the Vz. 58V was a close-range weapon. Thinking that he might have to reach out and touch someone at longer ranges, Bolan chose a Dragunov SVD-S sniper's rifle with a folding stock and standard PSO-1 telescopic sight. The piece was chambered in 7.62×54 R—the *R* standing for *Russian*—and in Bolan's expert hands it could bag targets out to fourteen hundred yards.

For heavy hitting when it counted, Bolan also bought a dozen URG-86 "universal" grenades, another Czech model combining both timed- and impact-fuse functions. Both were activated two seconds after release of the grenade's safety lever. From that point onward, any impact would produce a detonation—or the lethal egg would go off on its own in 4.6 seconds. Each URG contained forty-two grams of high explosive, with a pre-fragmented casing to ensure distribution of death on the fly.

The rest came down to odds and ends. Spare magazines and extra ammunition, a suppressor for the ALFA's threaded muzzle and a black steel reproduction of the famous Mark I trench knife widely issued in the First World War. Bolan paid for the mobile arsenal and duffel bags to hold the varied items using cash donated by a pimp in Baltimore who had no further use for money, velvet suits or the vintage purple Caddy Coupe de Ville he'd driven until very recently.

Under the circumstances, Bolan thought his contribution was appropriate.

And he would put it to good use.

BOXING HAD BEEN ASSOCIATED with the underworld for generations in America, and Bolan guessed it must have been the same in Europe. Violent men engaged in blood sport, managed—if not owned outright—by men whose penchant for mayhem made anything done in the ring seem G-rated and tame. Farther east, it was the same for wrestlers in Bulgaria, as Bolan understood it—and, in fact, the term *wrestler* had come to denote *mobster.* Then again, so had *businessman,* proving that no field of human endeavor was safe.

At one time or another, Bolan had been called upon to cleanse them all.

Approaching Oskar's gym, he saw a light burning upstairs, third floor, behind a pane of frosted glass. No view inside from where he stood. He found the metal staircase bolted to the back wall, accessed from an alley lined with trash cans, strewn with rubbish that had never made it to a bin.

Bolan had a choice. He could go in through the back door, which he found locked, or climb the fire escape and pick a window, maybe hope for entry from the roof as an alternative. He'd never seen an urban tenement that didn't have some kind of rooftop access from inside. The question was: What kind of access, and how well secured would it turn out to be?

The back door Bolan faced was steel and double-locked, a dead bolt and a keyhole in the doorknob. He could likely pick the latter with no problem, but the dead bolt would take longer, if his picks could open it at all. If there were other locks or bolts inside that Bolan couldn't see, it would be wasted time and effort, leaving him exposed and perhaps attracting someone from the inside who'd object to uninvited visitors.

That left the fire escape.

He jumped to grab its lowest section, seven feet above ground level, pulled it down and grimaced at the squeal of rusty metal. Bolan waited one full minute for the racket to evoke a curious reaction, then began to climb when no one showed. It didn't mean the noise had gone unnoticed, but at least security for Oskar's gym did not include a swift-response team for the alley.

On the second floor—which Europeans call the first, distinguished from the ground floor—Bolan found the windows painted over on the inside. Also locked, which made him wish he'd brought a glass cutter along. Too late to worry over that, and he moved on to find the same precautions against spying on the next two floors. He listened at the topmost windows, on the floor where he had seen light from the building's street side, but heard nothing to betray human inhabitants.

So, they were quiet at the moment. Or they'd moved the hostage, possibly disposed of him by this time. There was a slim chance, Bolan calculated, that the address he'd been given had been wrong from the beginning, though he doubted it. The only thing to do was to proceed and find a way inside. See who—if anyone—was home and what they had to tell him if he asked persuasively.

A Bolan specialty.

The roof was flat, with two old-fashioned television aerials protruding from the northeast and the southwest corners. Roughly in the middle stood a boxy structure resembling an outhouse, which he knew would grant him access to a flight of stairs descending to the tenement's top floor. That door was locked as well, of course, but Bolan jimmied it with his knife blade and seconds later breathed the pent-up atmosphere of Oskar's gym.

It smelled like sweat, leather and canvas, mildew and some kind of astringent.

Maybe just a whiff of blood.

And then, a sound. It was a man's voice, distant in relation to the place where Bolan stood, growling what could have been a question. Seconds later, in the place of a response, there came a gasping cry of pain.

Drawing his pistol, Bolan started down the stairs.

EMIL REISZ WAS TIRED. His fists ached, even though he'd worn a pair of lightweight boxing gloves while hammering the prisoner. His punches had been interspersed with questions that—so far—had gone unanswered but for curses. It was time to pass the gloves, he thought. Let Alois or Ladislav try their hands with the sphinx who would say nothing.

Or, perhaps they ought to try some other tools.

There'd be a mess to clean up afterward, but Oskar's gym had seen its share of blood over the years. A bit more wouldn't change the ambience significantly. Truth be told, it might help some of Oskar's fighters find their courage for a change.

In fact, they didn't need much information from the prisoner. Reisz knew his name and where he'd come from, not to mention *why* he'd come. No secret there. But orders had come down to find out whether anyone had helped the fool in transit, fed him any inside details of their operation to support his hopeless quest. If there was someone else behind him, sponsoring the effort, measures would be taken to eliminate that threat.

But only if they could obtain the names.

And so far, nothing.

He was fluent in profanity, this one. During the ordeal of interrogation he had cursed them up and down in English, German, Russian, not forgetting to include their mothers, grandmothers and all the smallest branches on their family trees. It was inspiring to a point, his tolerance for pain, the grim defiance even when he must have known he was as good as dead.

But then, beyond that point, it just became a tiresome exercise. Reisz thought he might as well be pounding steak for dinner. That way, at the very least, his efforts would produce a meal instead of aching knuckles.

Time for pliers, possibly. Or a truck battery with alligator clips.

Reisz checked his watch after he had removed the boxing gloves. Another fifteen minutes until change of shift, but their replacements could arrive any second. Let them pick up where he'd failed, and if some criticism fell upon him, then so be it. Three days, and no one else had managed to wring answers from the stubborn *piča* they had duct-taped to a straight-backed wooden chair between the third floor's pair of fighting rings.

If Reisz was criticized, there would be plenty of blame to go around.

"Enough for me," he told his two companions standing by. "Somebody want to have another go at him before we leave?"

"Forget it," Alois Perina said. "Let Jiří and his men finish the job."

"And mop up when they're done," Ladislav Seldon said.

"Suits me," Reisz answered as he tossed the bloodied gloves aside. "I think he's nearly finished, anyway."

"If there was someone else behind him, he'd have said by now," Perina opined.

"Probably," Reisz said, still not convinced. "I doubt we'll see this one again, regardless."

"And good riddance," Seldon said.

"All right, who wants a drink?" Reisz asked.

"What are we celebrating?" Perina asked.

"Who needs an excuse?" Seldon chimed in. "Make mine a double."

Reisz was moving toward the liquor cupboard, something that had always struck him as incongruous for a gymnasium, when he was suddenly distracted by a shadow in the doorway to his left. Jiří arriving early for a change, he thought, instead of twenty minutes late as usual. But when he turned to face the door, Reisz did not recognize the man who occupied the space.

He was tall and well-proportioned, dressed in dark clothes, with a solemn face that Reisz was sure he'd never seen before. Vaguely Italian in its aspect, but that could mean anything or nothing. More important was the pistol in his hand.

"What's wrong with you, Emil?" Perina asked, then tracked his gaze to spot the stranger watching them. Reisz didn't have to issue any orders. All three reached for guns at once, Reisz hoping he could draw his own before the grim-faced prowler fired.

BOLAN HAD NOT ATTACHED the ALFA's silencer before he left his hired car for the trek to Oskar's gym. It didn't matter at this late hour, on the top floor of a gym surrounded by commercial buildings that had shut down for the night.

He shot the seeming leader of the three men first, drilling his chest an inch or so off-center from a range of twenty feet. The guy went down without a whimper, slack and boneless when he hit the concrete floor. It seemed to take his backup by surprise, but neither faltered in attempts to pull their weapons.

Bolan ducked and tagged the shooter on his right, who seemed to be the faster of the two remaining on their feet. Not quite a perfect shot, but Bolan saw him lurch and stagger from the impact, then lose his footing, tumbling. If he managed to recover, it would cost him precious time, and Bolan used that breather to take care of number three.

The last man had his weapon drawn, some kind of automatic with a shiny stainless frame and blue-steel slide, maybe a Czech CZ 75. The piece was moving into target acquisition when the third round out of Bolan's ALFA struck its owner just below his left eye socket, snapping back his head and ruining his aim forever. Even then, the dead man got a shot off as he toppled over backward, setting free a rain of plaster dust from overhead.

Bolan rose from his crouch, surveyed the fallen and discovered that the second man he'd shot was still alive. Crossing the room to reach him, Bolan kicked his gun away and made a quick assessment of his wound. It would be fatal without treatment, but he couldn't pin it to a deadline. Rather than take chances, Bolan put another .40 S&W round between the shooter's eyes and finished it.

That done, he moved to stand before the bloody figure of a man dressed in only a pair of boxer shorts, secured to a wooden chair by strips of silver duct tape wrapped around his torso, wrists and ankles. He was conscious, barely, using some reserve of energy to hold his head up, watching Bolan through the one eye that wasn't swollen shut. Mouth-breathing since his nose was flattened from repeated blows.

Bolan knelt on concrete, outside the ring of blood spatters, and peered into the mottled face, which at present was barely recognizable from photographs he'd seen before he left the States. Playing it safe, he leaned in closer and addressed the human punching bag.

"Andrew Murton?"

The head bobbed once, then sank onto the captive's chest. Bolan worked quickly with his knife, slitting the duct tape, peeling it away. There was no way to spare the prisoner that ripping pain, but Murton barely seemed to feel it.

"Clothes?" Bolan asked.

Murton nodded vaguely to his left and answered, "Ober dere."

Bolan recovered shirt, slacks, socks and loafers from a corner of the gym and brought them back to Murton, helped him dress himself, acutely conscious of the fact that they were wasting precious time. Whether his gunshots had been noted in the seedy neighborhood or not, there was a chance that reinforcements might arrive at any moment. If that happened…

Murton wobbled on his feet as Bolan held him upright, then took baby steps in the direction of the exit. "Godda go," he said. "Somebud comin'."

Bolan didn't question that, assuming there'd been some form of communication with his captors during Murton's ordeal, or that Murton had a rough idea of when new torturers arrived to spell the old. Whatever, it was time for them to hit the street.

The prisoner would need a medic, then they'd need to talk

about the *other* prisoner whom Bolan had been sent to rescue, if that still was possible. In either case, his job was half-done, more or less.

If they could only make it back to Bolan's car alive.

He helped Murton limp down three flights of stairs to the ground floor, led him to the main street exit and unlocked it from inside. The cool night air seemed to refresh Murton a little, helped him to pick up his lagging pace. They'd covered half a block when headlights washed across them, from behind. Doors slammed, and Murton turned back toward the sound.

"Shid!" he exclaimed. "Run now!"

Bolan glanced back in time to see four new arrivals on the sidewalk, staring after them and jabbering together, one of them already reaching underneath his jacket for a weapon.

Murton had it right.

Run now!

2

Half carrying the man he'd rescued moments earlier—one-ninety if he weighed an ounce—Bolan reached the nearest corner, ducked around it and stopped there. Propped Murton up against the rough brick wall and peered back toward the place they'd come from, gun in hand.

"Why stoppen?" Murton asked him, slurring.

"To see if I can end it here," Bolan replied, his index finger on the ALFA's trigger.

But it wasn't meant to play that way, apparently. Instead of giving chase, the four goons from the car—it could have been a Citroën, maybe something manufactured locally—were piling back into their vehicle. It bought Bolan a little time, but precious little. And none to waste on conversation with a man who was barely conscious.

Bolan made his choice. He half crouched and drove his shoulder into Murton's gut, already bruised and aching. With a *whoof!* the battered man slumped over Bolan's shoulder, perfectly positioned for a fireman's carry. Bolan flexed his legs and bore the weight, turned toward the nearby darkened side street where he'd left his Volvo S80 and broke into the fastest run that he could manage under the circumstances.

It reminded him of combat on another battlefield, retrieving wounded comrades under fire. He'd always done his best to keep faith with the Special Forces credo that no soldier stays behind. That wasn't always possible, of course—sometimes you had to make the choice of dying with a corpse or moving on to fight another day—but his record was better than average.

And leaving Murton alive with the men who'd abducted him wasn't an option.

Bolan heard an engine growling as he reached the Volvo, used its tab to pop the door locks from a distance, and upon reaching the vehicle he began the chore of putting Murton in a seat. He chose the rear, where Murton could lie down and be out of sight, though not entirely safe from any bullets slicing through the Volvo's coachwork. At the very least, a backseat ride would keep him out of Bolan's lap and clear from Bolan's line of fire.

Murton cooperated to the best of his ability, huffing and groaning as he rolled onto the Volvo's rear bench seat and drawing in his legs as Bolan slammed the door. A quick dash to the driver's side, key twist, ignore the chime that warned him of a shoulder harness left unfastened, and they pulled out from the curb just as the other car found them with its headlights, closing in.

The Volvo's five-speed automatic transmission left both of Bolan's hands free for driving—or for fighting, if it came to that. The duffel bags containing most of his new weapons were concealed in the sedan's trunk, out of reach for the moment, but he still had the ALFA autoloader with nine rounds remaining and four extra magazines secured in pockets. If he couldn't stop the chase car and its occupants with fifty-three live rounds… well, then, what good was he?

But Bolan's first choice was evasion and escape.

He'd killed three men already, in their lair at Oskar's gym, but that was vastly different than a running firefight through the streets of Prague. Even at night, the city never really slept. A fair share of its approximately 1.2 million inhabitants had work to do at any hour of the day or night, including a municipal police department with fifteen district headquarters spotted around the 192-square-mile metro area. He could meet one of their silver Škoda Octavia prowl cars at any turn, and since his private code barred any use of deadly force against police, most of his options would be lost in that event.

He drove without a plan so far, aware that he was winding toward Old Town, the ancient heart of Prague where early settlers had put down roots nearly twelve hundred years ago. It was the last place where he wanted to be trapped, surrounded by the landmarks that drew tourists, with a greater likelihood of meeting the police, and so he scrolled a street map of the city that he'd memorized while he was airborne, seeking options.

If he had it right, they were about to exit Prague 5—one of Prague's twenty-two administrative districts—and enter Prague 4, specifically a suburb known as Kunratice. If he could lose the Citroën in its winding streets, so much the better. And if not…

It would be time for drastic action.

JIŘÍ KOSTKA CLUTCHED his pistol tight enough to make his knuckles ache, bracing his free hand on the Citroën's dashboard as they swerved around another corner, entering a residential street. The Volvo they were chasing showed no signs of slowing down, so Kostka snapped an order at his driver, Ivan Durych.

"Overtake them, will you? If you can't do that, pull over now and let me drive!"

"This is a DS4," Durych reminded him, keeping his eyes locked on the target. "Not a goddamned Maserati."

"Can you get us within shooting distance, or is that too much to ask?" Kostka demanded.

"Don't you think I'm trying?"

"Well, stop trying, then, and do it!"

Kostka realized his anger was misplaced, but he was known for his explosive temper, one of several qualities that had resulted in his elevation to the post of squad leader within the Werich syndicate. Unlike some blowhards he had met, Kostka's bite was worse than his bark, a fact well recognized by everyone who knew him. He would strike without a second thought and kill without remorse.

So why, in God's name, had he let the runners slip away from him outside Oskar's gym?

Something about the tall man, when he turned to glare at Kostka on the sidewalk, had persuaded Kostka in a heartbeat that they would be wise to let him think he had escaped, then run him down and kill him while his back was turned, and either retrieve their prisoner or eliminate him at the same time. That would leave important questions still unanswered, but Kostka thought that was preferable to the American's escape.

No one could blame him for the breakout. That would fall on Emil Reisz—who, if he had an ounce of luck at all, was lying dead at the gymnasium with his two stooges. Kostka had been early to relieve Reisz, and for that reason alone had caught the prisoner and his still-unknown benefactor at the scene. Five minutes later, and they would have gotten clean away.

Still, if he lost them, there would be no one else Kostka could blame. They were in hot pursuit, well armed, but if they could not salvage the debacle *he* would be the loser. Might wish he was dead himself when time came to deliver the bad news.

Just make it right, he thought, and hissed at Durych with a fresh demand for speed.

"We're gaining," Durych snapped. "Be ready!"

In the backseat, Kostka heard his other soldiers—Michal Lobkovic and Zdeněk Vojan—cocking pistols. They were both fair shots, but Kostka didn't like the thought of either firing past him from the rear while they were racing through the streets. Half turning in his seat, he said, "Be careful if there's shooting. I don't want a goddamned bullet in my ear from one of you!"

Vojan grinned back at him and said, "I never shot a man by accident."

"Let's keep it that way," Kostka answered, turning back to watch the Volvo as it swung around another corner, vanishing from sight.

"Will you—"

"I know," Durych said, interrupting him. "Speed up! Get closer! Work a miracle!"

"I need a driver, not a priest!" said Kosta.

"Hold on!" Durych warned as they reached the corner, rounding it in a skid that was barely controlled.

Cursing came from the backseat as momentum threw Vojan and Lobkovic together for a second, banging shoulders. Kostka powered down his window, sight wind whipping at his face and ruffling his short hair as he thrust his shooting arm outside the car. Another half block closer, and he could attempt a shot. One of the rear tires, or perhaps the driver, if he got a lucky break.

Where was the passenger? Kostka saw nothing of him, guessed that he was probably slumped over, maybe rolling in the backseat. Either way, it helped to have him clear of any shot that Kostka tried to make. Retrieving him alive would be a bonus; catching *both* runners alive would be sweet icing on the cake.

But he would settle for a pair of corpses if it was the only way to stop them.

Dead men couldn't answer questions, but neither could they squeal to the police.

ANOTHER BLOCK, and Bolan heard a heavy, restless shifting in the seat behind him. Glancing in the rearview mirror, he saw Andrew Murton's head block out the glare of headlights from the chase car.

"Better stay down," he advised his passenger. "They could start shooting anytime."

"Ah wanna hep."

"You want to help?" Bolan said. "Lie back down so I can use the mirror."

"Gimme guh."

Not likely, Bolan thought. The last thing that he needed was a punch-drunk shooter blasting out the Volvo's windows, peppering the houses that lined both sides of the street.

"I say again—"

He saw the muzzle-flash before his lips could form the order, jigged the steering wheel and knew they'd literally dodged a bullet in the night.

"Get down!" Bolan barked, relieved to see the shadow figure in his mirror disappear. Bolan knew Murton had endured an ordeal that would break a lesser man, but that would not prevent him from knocking Murton cold if it became a matter of survival.

One more muzzle-flash from the pursuit car, just as Bolan swerved into a side street on his left. Again, the shot went wild, buzzing away to who knew where. With any luck, the slug would strike a tree trunk or an empty vehicle. The flip side was a bedroom wall or window pierced, a sleeper shocked awake by sudden agony—or never waking up at all.

The hunters didn't give a damn about potential bystanders. They had a job to do and they were focused on it to the exclusion of all else. Professionals. Nothing but victory or death would stop them.

Bolan was determined that they would not win.

Which left one option.

First, he had to find a killing ground that minimized the prospects of collateral damage. There, if he could locate such a place before a bullet found one of the Volvo's tires, its fuel tank or its engine block, he'd make a stand and see what came of it.

Back to the map he'd memorized from the internet. Off to the east, three-quarters of a mile or so, the Vltava River surged against its banks, the waterfront including warehouses for cargo shipped by barge from Germany and Austria. Deliveries might be ongoing at this hour, but the traffic should be relatively light, and there would be no tourists loitering around the docks to serve as targets in a shooting gallery.

The chase car lost a little ground to Bolan on the turn but soon began to make it up again. He gave the driver credit, wishing at the same time that he'd blow a gasket, have a heart attack, whatever might truncate the chase without a battle to attract police.

Too late, he thought.

Some neighborhoods of Prague might tolerate a shot or two around midnight, but Kunratice did not strike him as one of those. If someone—make that *several* someones—hadn't called the cops already, Bolan would be very much surprised. That thought turned up the ticktock volume of the numbers falling in his mind, but Bolan dialed it back again and focused on his half-formed plan.

If he could—

Hold on, what was this? Another pair of headlights coming up behind the chase car, not dawdling like a local coming home after a night out on the town. He couldn't call it a pursuit, at least not yet. There were no flashing lights, no siren to suggest an officer behind the wheel.

A second chase car? Reinforcements summoned via cell phone or some other means to help the first team close their trap? If that were true, there might be anywhere from two to five or six guns in the second vehicle. The odds against survival may have doubled.

And what difference did it make?

Bolan had never been a quitter, knew the meaning of surrender but had never practiced it. Eight guns—or even ten—made life more difficult, definitely. But he had beaten worse odds in the past and walked away from the situation. The bottom line: even if death was certain for himself and his companion, he would fight until his last round had been fired, then take it hand to hand. Unless they dropped him with a lucky shot, the hunting party's scarred survivors would not soon forget their meeting with The Executioner.

He might even return to haunt them in their dreams.

"WE HAVE A TAIL," Durych announced to no one in particular.

Kostka spun in his seat so quickly that he strained his neck and almost yelped at the onslaught of sudden, piercing pain. He saw headlights behind them, clearly following the Citroën.

"Who is it?" he demanded.

"*Do prdele!* How should I know?" Durych answered sharply.

"Not the *policajti*," Vojan offered. "They'd have lit their Christmas tree by now."

"Friends of the one we're chasing, maybe," Lobkovic suggested, sounding worried.

"Only joining in just now?" Kostka replied, half speaking to himself. "Where have they been?"

"Who cares?" Vojan retorted. "Do you want me to get rid of them?"

"Not yet. The one we want's still in the car ahead. But watch them and be ready if they try to overtake us."

Kostka wondered if he ought to call for help, but how would he explain the situation? Truth be told, he couldn't say exactly where they were, so asking for a backup team would be superfluous. He wished they'd come prepared with more than pistols—automatic rifles, maybe shotguns—but it didn't help.

What was the old saying? *"Bez peněz do hospody nelez."*

Without money do not go to the pub.

Translation: Be prepared. You have to pay to play.

And who thought up this stuff? Likely someone who'd bitten off more than he could chew but lived to tell about it afterward.

Kostka could only hope he'd have the same good luck. One thing was certain, though. If he broke off the chase from fear of being trapped, his end was certain. When he took the story back to Lida Werich he would find no mercy waiting for him. Failure was not tolerated. It would certainly not be tolerated, much less favored with an amnesty.

And if survival was not one of Kostka's options, he would choose the quick death of a bullet over anything that Werich might devise to punish him. No contest there. Be sure to save a bullet for himself, in case it all went wrong.

"They're heading for the river," Durych said.

"The river? Why?"

"I'm not a *zasranej* mind reader, am I?"

Kostka nearly pistol-whipped him then, but that would be the same as suicide, the speed at which they were traveling. Instead, he satisfied himself with muttered curses, leaning from his open window to attempt another shot.

And missed, of course. Just as he squeezed the CZ's trigger, his intended target made another sharp turn, this one to the right, and Kostka's bullet screamed away downrange to find some unknown point of impact in the night. As Durych made the turn, Kostka could see the waterfront ahead of them.

He smelled the river, with its scent of dead fish, diesel fuel and dreams vanished downstream.

"Maybe he has a boat," Durych said.

"Then we have to stop him now," Kostka replied, "before he gets aboard and goes somewhere that we can't follow."

"*Jo, jo.* I'm working on it!"

"So, work harder!"

"Seru na tvojí matku!" Durych snapped, but stood on the accelerator, somehow wringing more speed from the growling Citroën. "Unless that crate can fly, we have them now!"

WITH SOMETHING LIKE a hundred yards of pavement left before he hit the water, Bolan made his move. It wasn't complex, but it still required precision timing, with coordination of the Volvo's brake and its accelerator. If he did it properly, the car would make a sharp one-eighty, wind up facing back in the direction they'd just come from, stopping with its high beams aimed into the chase-car driver's face. And if he blew it, they'd go tumbling ass-over-teakettle down the dock, hammered unconscious—maybe dead—before they plunged into the water.

One chance. But that was all a soldier could expect.

"Hang on!" he warned his backseat rider, hoping Murton had the sense and strength to brace himself. A wrong move, and it wouldn't matter if he picked up any more new bruises.

But it worked. The Volvo nosed down, slowing sharply, and began to fishtail just as Bolan cranked the steering wheel hard left and stamped on the accelerator. By the time it came to rest again, four heartbeats later, he was facing toward the chase car with the ALFA in his left hand, out the open driver's window, while his right hand gripped the wheel. Behind him, Murton mumbled something like a curse, and Bolan let it pass.

He watched the two cars bearing down upon him, closing fast. The first, with four opponents the big American had already seen, was in his sights. The second, still an unknown quantity, was bringing up the rear, joining the play for reasons Bolan hadn't grasped yet. Nine rounds in the ALFA, and he could reload in seconds flat if he was free and clear. Driving at speed would complicate the process, but—

Bolan attacked, gunning the Volvo forward on a clear collision course and rapid-firing with the ALFA autoloader. Three, four, five rounds through the chase car's windshield as the gap between them narrowed. Then his enemy was swerving off to Bolan's left, plowing into a trailer clearly built for catering, its drab facade showing a poor painted rendition of a sausage on a bun.

That left one car in line, and Bolan wouldn't fire on it until he had at least a rough fix on its occupants. The Volvo's high beams only showed him one man in the vehicle, but what did that prove? Bolan had no friends in Prague—this might be a cop off duty, maybe working undercover, or a journalist who stumbled on the chase by sheer coincidence. Maybe a stupid rubbernecker with more curiosity than common sense. Shooting him first and asking questions later did not mesh with Bolan's modus operandi.

So he brought the Volvo to another squealing hault, leaped out, keeping his car between himself and the third vehicle, finally recognizable as an Audi A4 sedan. It braked in turn, the driver stepping out with no one else behind him. Watching Bolan carefully, the last arrival circled his own car, approached the Citroën and peered inside. He pulled a flashlight from a pocket of his windbreaker and played its beam around inside the car.

Blood on the dash and windshield. Huddled, vaguely human shapes.

He straightened, said something in Czech. Stood waiting for an answer until Bolan told him, "Sorry. Failure to communicate."

"American?" the stranger asked, his English sharply accented. When Bolan offered no reply, he said, "You've killed the driver, and it looks as though his friend up front may have a broken neck. These two," he went on, waving vaguely toward the backseat, "could wake up at any time."

Bolan still couldn't read the stranger, so he asked, "You want me to take care of that?"

"It's better if we leave them as they are, I think. They'll have a devil of a time explaining this. It ought to be amusing."

Bolan watched the stranger moving toward him, held his ALFA lowered but prepared for instant action. "This is your idea of humor?" he inquired.

The Audi's driver shrugged. "Not normally, but I have learned to find amusement where I can," he said. "One never knows when life may suddenly present a spectacle."

"And you just happen to be there," Bolan said.

"Ah. It was not a coincidence. I think you understand this, eh?"

"It's sinking in," Bolan replied.

The stranger's draw was smooth and fast, his pistol aimed at Bolan's forehead even as the ALFA centered on his chest.

"And now, what you would call the punch line, I believe," he said. "You are under arrest."

3

Baltimore, Maryland
Two days earlier

The sixth victim, another working girl, had been discovered floating in the Chesapeake off Locust Point, near Fort Henry. As with the five preceding kills, her throat was slashed back to the spine, a case of near decapitation after a savage beating and a list of signature indignities well recognized by homicide investigators. FBI agents were working on the case, inspiring all the usual resentment from embarrassed local cops. The newspapers and smiling TV anchors babbled on about a "Ripper" in their midst, a stalker who had psych profilers baffled.

The truth, as usual, was rather different.

At Baltimore P.D., they knew that all six victims were employed—read *owned*—by Luscious Luther Johnson. Thirty-six years old, imprisoned twice for pandering and living off the proceeds of prostitution, Johnson was an aging dog who'd never managed to learn any new tricks on the street or in the joint. He liked controlling women, playing God in lives blighted by sexual abuse and drugs. He liked the money, too, of course, but that was secondary to the kick he got from reigning over female serfs.

Before his second prison term, Luther had disciplined unruly girls with belt lashings, a wire coat hanger sometimes, but nothing permanent. Something had changed inside him while he served his time at Roxbury Correctional, perhaps a hard-ening of attitude precipitated by the fact that two of Luther's "bitches" had been brave enough to testify against him at his trial. One of them left the state thereafter, while the other kept working the streets around Patterson Park as if she hadn't a care in the world.

Big mistake.

Divine Jones had been first in the series, succeeded by others who balked at the offer to join Johnson's stable or held back too much of the cash they'd received from their johns. No disrespect of any sort was tolerated.

Police had questioned Luther at least a dozen times so far. But *knowing* he was probably involved and *proving* it were very different things. A team from Vice had worked on putting Johnson back in stir for pimping, using Maryland's three-strikes law to send him up for life, but Luscious Luther wasn't quite as careless as he'd been in the past. He kept no records of illicit business, paid his taxes on a chain of coin-op laundries and had generally kept his nose clean in the public eye.

Bolan had been passing through "Charm City"—also known to some as "Mobtown"—with no plans to hang around beyond a night's rest at a local Motel 6, when he heard about the case on CNN. He'd made a couple calls, stayed over for an extra night of observation on the scene and saw a chance to do some good.

Like any other pimp who has a thriving urban racket, Johnson paid his dues. He tithed religiously to the Peruzzi family, which Bolan thought might rate a visit at some future date, along with bagmen from the Baltimore P.D. and City Hall. None would protect him if the Feds collected evidence to try him as a six-time psycho killer, but until that evidence appeared Johnson was golden.

And he wasn't hard to find.

His second night in Baltimore, Bolan had followed Johnson on the pimp's rounds, collecting cash from go-betweens, glad-handing people who appeared to be his friends, drinking at half a dozen bars where songs with indecipherable lyrics threatened long-term hearing loss. Bolan was on him when he spent an hour with his number-one old lady at her place, waiting for Johnson in the shadows when the man emerged.

From that point on, Johnson's night of celebration went downhill. His bluster vanished with a glimpse of Bolan's cold eyes and a close look at the sleek Beretta in his fist. Disarmed and cuffed with plastic zip ties, Johnson had directed Bolan to a small apartment that he called his bank. Inside it, with his hands freed to accommodate the combination lock on a wall safe beside a small desk, he'd given up roughly a quarter-million dollars gleaned from others' suffering and degradation, smiling all the while.

"I jus' keep that aroun' for incidentals, yo. Man like you'self know how it is."

"You're right," Bolan replied. "I do."

"So, we good here, o' what?"

"Almost. About the women…"

"R*iii*ght. You want a lady now? I'd say you can afford a fine one."

"The six women that you killed."

"Whoa, man! You trippin' now. Pigs axed me all about that, and I done been cleared, awight?"

"Well," Bolan said, "there's cleared, and then there's *cleared.*"

"Man, what you tryin' to say?" Johnson asked, trying to prolong the conversation as he quickly reached into an open drawer of the desk and pulled out a small gun.

But Bolan was faster with his response, letting the Beretta speak for him, with one sharp word that brooked no contradiction. Johnson hit the deep shag carpet with a look of dazed surprise in all three eyes, shivered a little, then lay still.

Bolan secured his loot, all hundred-dollar bills, in a valise he borrowed from the late and unlamented pimp, locked the pad behind him and was on his way downstairs when the soft vibration of his cell phone took him by surprise. No more than half a dozen people in the world had Bolan's number. He had never fallen prey to random telemarketers.

A quick check on the screen showed him that it was Hal Brognola calling from his office at the Justice Building in D.C., well past the normal span of business hours.

"Go," Bolan said without preamble.

"How soon can you be here?" Brognola asked. "Well, let's say Arlington."

"I'm forty miles away," Bolan said, "give or take."

"I'll see you there," the big Fed said. "ASAP."

BROGNOLA DIDN'T HAVE TO specify which "there" he had in mind. They'd met on previous occasions at Arlington National Cemetery, and while that facility closed to the public from 8:00 p.m. to 7:00 a.m., there was an all-night restaurant on Marshall Drive, near the U.S. Marine Corps War Memorial, that served as backup outside of visiting hours. Bolan found Brognola's Buick Regal CXL already waiting in the parking lot when he rolled in, his second-oldest living friend ensconced with coffee at a corner booth.

"You made good time," Brognola said in greeting.

"It wasn't all that far," Bolan replied, taking his seat across from the man.

A red-haired waitress came and took their breakfast order, filled a coffee cup for Bolan, then retreated.

"So, what's the squeal?" Bolan asked, when they were alone.

"It may upset your appetite," Brognola said.

"Try me."

"Okay. What do you know about the child-sex trade?"

"Broad strokes," Bolan replied. "It's global. There's a UN protocol designed to stop it, written ten or twelve years back, ratified by something like a hundred countries all around the world."

"One hundred seventeen," Brognola said. "For all the good it does."

"No teeth in that, of course," Bolan continued, "but most countries have their own laws penalizing human trafficking, child prostitution and pornography."

"Again," Brognola said, "for all the good they do."

A nod from Bolan as he said, "Enforcement's spotty, sure. Big money in the trade, and some of that sticks to official hands."

"You've heard of child-sex tourism, I guess," he said.

"Junkets for pedophiles," Bolan replied. "They catch a flight to someplace where the cops and courts are paid to shut their eyes."

"That's it in a nutshell," Brognola granted. "Fifteen years ago, the International Labor Organization estimated that child-sex tourism produced two to fourteen percent of the gross domestic product for half a dozen Asian countries—Thailand, the Philippines, India, Malaysia, Indonesia. Since then, it's been picking up in Mexico, Central America and Eastern Europe. The U.K. and the States have laws in place to punish nationals who go abroad to prey on children, but it's tough to make the charges stick."

Bolan had dealt with human traffickers before and rated them among the lowest forms of parasites, but shutting down the trade was an impossibility. As long as there were customers with cash in hand, there'd be suppliers to provide whatever they desired.

"Go on," he urged Brognola.

"So, let's flash back to the so-called Velvet Revolution. Nineteen eighty-nine," Brognola said. "Czechoslovakia divides into the Czech Republic and Slovakia. Assume they've always had their share of hookers. Overnight, the business takes off like a house on fire. The Czech Republic's parliament banned any kind of organized sex trade—brothels, pimping, anything that smells like mob involvement—but they left the working girls alone, free to work under license. The net result—last year, reporters counted eight hundred sixty dedicated brothels nationwide, with two hundred in Prague. Hookers advertise in the newspaper classifieds section, charging an average sixty dollars an hour."

"Someone's greased the cops," Bolan said. No surprise.

"Big-time," Brognola said. "Two years ago, the state police investigated thirty suspected traffickers. Prosecutors took nineteen to trial and convicted a dozen. Facing maximum terms of twelve to fifteen years, three were sent up for three-to-five. The other nine had their sentences suspended and are back in business as we speak."

"It sounds familiar," Bolan said, thinking of every place where organized corruption put down roots. And that meant *everywhere*.

"Getting back to the kids," Brognola said, "they come into Prague from all over. Eastern Europe and the Balkans, on to Vietnam and China. Some pass through the Czech Republic on their way to operations in the West, and others never make it out. If they survive, they'll age into the adult trade or wind up on the streets, burned out and drug addicted, living hand to mouth."

"This must be going somewhere," Bolan said.

"You're right. It is. Seems like the scumbags aren't content to buy their kids from so-called parents anymore. It still goes on, of course, especially in Asia and some parts of South America, but kidnapping is cheaper. Why fly buyers halfway round the world, when you can cruise the streets of Prague, Brno or Ostrava and snatch them off the sidewalk? Slash your operating costs on one hand—on the other, keep enough white kids in stock to balance out the ethnic inventory. It's a win-win situation for the sons of bitches."

"And?" Bolan knew there was more to come.

"And," Brognola replied, "that brings us to the reason why we're here."

THE WAITRESS BROUGHT their meals, topped off their coffee mugs and went away. Brognola pushed his scrambled eggs around the plate, sampled a piece of toast, then set it down.

"Last week—four days ago, to be precise—somebody grabbed a ten-year-old girl in Prague. Her name is Mandy Murton. She's American."

"Odd place to find her," Bolan said.

"School trip, if you can believe it," Hal answered. "It's the sort of thing rich parents do these days, I'm told. Instead of summer school or family vacation time, you send the kiddies off to Europe or wherever in a small, select group with teachers from their private schools as guides, tutors and chaperones. Supposedly, most of the trips come off without a hitch, aside from minor illness now and then."

"But this one didn't."

"Right. It's still unclear what happened to the girl, exactly," Brognola went on. "Another kid swears Mandy wasn't taken from the room they shared. Seems she went out to get a Coke instead of calling room service. The vending machines are on alternate floors, so she had to go up or down one. She never came back."

"Security cameras?" Bolan asked.

"The hotel's equipped," the big Fed confirmed. "Exits and elevators covered, but it's spotty on the hallways. There's no tape of Mandy leaving, on her own or with an escort. Two things clicked as possibles. First up, a food delivery around that time, downstairs, with crates of goodies coming in and empties going out. Second, a bellhop with his face averted from the CCTV, wheeling out a laundry cart."

"How many people on the food delivery?" Bolan asked.

"Two came with the truck," Brognola said. "A couple from the kitchen helped them with unloading."

"Have they been cleared?"

Brognola shrugged and tried the toast again, then answered with his mouth full. "They've been *questioned* by the cops in Prague and by the PCR—those are the Feds, Police of the Czech Republic. No evidence of any criminal activity has been discovered, quote, unquote."

"The faceless bellhop, then."

"More likely," Brognola agreed. "A shot, some chloroform,

a blackjack—take your pick. One guy could shift a ten-year-old without backup, much less involving two hotel employees."

"So, she's gone," Bolan said. "Four days, Hal."

"I know, I know. There's been no ransom call, so that's a wash. Whoever snatched the girl had other things in mind. Whether it was a trafficker or just some random psycho off the street, it's all bad news."

Bolan tried to decide which might be worse and couldn't make the call.

"I don't know what to tell you. It's a heartbreaker."

"I hear you," Brognola replied. "But here's the rub—her daddy is a well-connected chief of corporate security at GenTex Oil. Any given year, he earns more than the President of the United States."

"He's making noise," Bolan surmised.

"I wish it were that simple," Brognola replied. "Before he took the GenTex job, he was a Navy SEAL for sixteen years. Won every decoration they could pin onto his wet suit, except the Congressional Medal of Honor, and that was a close call. On his last time out—in Pakistan, no less—he saved a wounded teammate's life. The other guy happened to be the grandson of a Texas senator with tons of GenTex stock in his portfolio."

"Which nailed his present job," Bolan observed. "A hero with connections."

"And with *skills,*" Brognola stressed. "He's not just making noise. When no one from the FBI, the Company or State could satisfy him, he went over there."

"By which you mean—"

"To Prague," Brognola said. "I shit you not. It's *Death Wish Seven,* or whatever, and the film crew isn't using blanks."

"Has there been contact?"

Brognola sipped his coffee, grimaced—too much sugar.

"There's no way to verify it," he told Bolan. "This guy—Andrew Murton—may be middle-aged and rusty, but he's still a player. Flew on bogus papers to the Czech Republic, and he likely has at least one spare ID on tap for when he's ready to come home. *If* he comes home."

Bolan waited for Brognola to tell it his way, in his own good time.

"Could he find guns in Prague?" the man from Justice asked rhetorically. "Hell, yes. Has there been trouble since he landed? Cops report that one suspected trafficker's gone missing, but he had a court appearance scheduled for next month. Could be a simple bail jumper. The thing is, Murton had been talking to his wife something like five, six times a day. Updating her, you know. And now he's stopped."

"How long?" Bolan asked.

"Half a day. It spooked her bad enough for her to call the Hoover Building. They reached out to me."

"And here we are," Bolan said.

"Right. What do you think?"

"About the girl? I told you, Hal—"

"I know. But what about the dad? If there's a chance that we could pull him out…"

"It plays out one of two ways," Bolan said. "He either found the traffickers who took his daughter, or he found somebody else. With option B, the only reason for not killing him straight up would be a ransom bid."

"Again, there's been no call," Brognola said.

"Okay. He's either dead or being held by someone with *another* reason not to put him down. Maybe interrogation. Maybe using him for leverage somewhere down the line."

"Bad news, no matter how you look at it," the man said.

"The worst," Bolan agreed.

"All right," Brognola said. "It's your call. Want to go and have a look around, or not?"

THE FLIGHT FROM Dulles International to Paris-Orly Airport spanned seven hours and forty-eight minutes. Orly to Prague consumed another hour, plus the downtime Bolan spent waiting to make his Czech Airlines connection. Bolan had used the time efficiently, to study Brognola's file on Andrew Murton, then erase it; to memorize the Google map of Prague; and finally, to catch up on the sleep he'd miss when he had reached his destination.

Finding Murton in the urban jungle that was Prague seemed like a nearly hopeless task to Bolan, but he knew that *nearly* wasn't absolute. Someone had seen the missing father. Someone knew what had become of him, whether he was alive or dead. Someone would talk, if the correct inducement was applied.

The problem: Bolan was a stranger to the Czech Republic and its capital, clearly a foreigner. Unlike the vanished former SEAL, he spoke neither German nor Russian, much less Czech, Slovak, Croatian or Bulgarian. The good news: according to his *Fodor's* guidebook, ten percent of all Czechs spoke at least some English. In Prague, the number supposedly rose to fifty percent for residents aged nineteen to thirty-five, and hit eighty percent for those eighteen or younger.

So all I have to do, he thought, *is keep asking directions from kids on the street.*

It was a joke at first, then soured on him when he thought about the people he was hunting and their chosen trade. Whether or not he could find Andrew Murton—much less the aggrieved father's child—Bolan vowed to wreak havoc among the Czech merchants of misery.

Scorched earth, if he could pull it off.

If not, at least a healthy dose of cleansing fire.

Bolan had never been a moralist per se. He didn't care who slept with whom, or why, as long as all concerned were consenting adults or roughly equal in age. He didn't mind if sex was sold or bartered, either. What repulsed him was the domination of illicit prostitution by a breed of predators who victimized the helpless to enrich themselves. Slave traders, in effect, and Bolan owed them nothing but a bullet, which, in most cases, was long years overdue.

He harbored no real hope of saving Mandy Murton. Even if he found her still alive, in Prague or somewhere else, and managed to extract her from the hell that had consumed her life of privilege, what would be left of her? Would years of therapy undo the trauma she had suffered at the hands of her abductors and their paying customers?

Bolan knew how her father must have felt. His own long war against the Mafia had started with a tragedy at home, akin to Andrew Murton's. Bolan had exacted justice on his own, using his military skills, when there'd been no one left to save. He didn't have to speculate over the depth of Murton's rage, the guilt that haunted him for failure to protect his own from half a world away.

He found that Brognola was right. It didn't take a master spy to find black-market guns in Prague. In fact, it only took a name and Luscious Luther Johnson's contribution to the cause. Bolan was pleased to spend the cash he'd taken from a killer pimp in aid of tracking and destroying other predators. If not exactly karma, it still felt like some kind of poetic justice.

As for information, that came down to asking questions. Brognola had gotten him started with the name of Murton's suspected first victim—an indicted trafficker, one Mikoláš Zeman. The vanished man had known associates, and Bolan, having duly armed himself beforehand, went in search of them.

The first, a twice-convicted brothel boss named Stanislav Karpíšek, managed to convince Bolan that he knew nothing.

The second, František Patočka, had avoided felony indictments to the present day, which proved that he was slick and knew the value of connections spanning both sides of the law. He didn't want to talk, took some persuading, but he'd finally admitted hearing that a certain rude American with strange ideas of justice had been causing ripples on the streets of Prague. Past tense, that was, since he'd been lured into a trap and neutralized.

Dead or alive?

Patočka couldn't say, but if his life depended on it he would have started seeking answers at a sweaty hole called Oskar's, where prizefighters, the *boxeprize bojovníci,* trained for their bouts under syndicate tutelage.

Bolan had thanked Patočka in the only way he could, after the thug came at him with a concealed knife—he released him from the distasteful toil of life. Then Bolan had moved on to see a man about a man at Oskar's gym. The rest was history, and he was staring down a pistol's muzzle with a badge behind it.

Busted, dead to rights.

4

"So, what now?" Bolan asked the cop who had him covered.

"First, I suppose, we introduce ourselves," the cop replied. "I am Jan Reynek, a sergeant in the PCR Agency for Organized Crime. You know the PCR, yes?"

Bolan nodded, thinking back to Hal Brognola's briefing. "Police of the Czech Republic," he said.

"That is correct," Reynek said. "I know your friend already," he continued, nodding toward the Volvo, where Murton was crawling from the backseat.

"He's had a rough couple of days," Bolan said.

"So I understand. His daughter even more so, possibly." Reynek's sharp eyes returned to Bolan's face. "And you are…?"

"Won't they cover all this at booking?" Bolan asked him.

Staying well beyond arm's reach, Reynek lowered his pistol. "I am undecided as to that," he said. "This case has… complications."

"Oh?"

"Indeed. Your name?"

"Matt Cooper."

"With papers to support it?"

"If you'd like to see them," Bolan answered.

"Maybe later. You're American, like Mr. Murton. Sent, no doubt, to rescue him where Czech police could not?"

"Before you take offense," Bolan replied, "that's how it played."

"You're right again. And I take no offense. Nor do I take responsibility for others when they fail. You represent the FBI? Perhaps the CIA?"

"Neither," Bolan answered. Walking on the razor's edge of truth as he said, "I'm a private contractor."

"Ah, Blackwater!"

"Without a private army or religious motivations," Bolan said.

"A purist. I salute you for succeeding where so many of my colleagues proved inadequate."

If that was meant as sarcasm, Reynek needed to work on his delivery. He'd come off sounding too sincere, a feeling reinforced by the expression on his dour face. He glanced back toward the Citroën, seeming relaxed and heedless of the ALFA autoloader still in Bolan's hand.

"These *kreténi,* I suppose, are Mr. Murton's kidnappers?"

"Some of them," Bolan said.

"Where might I find the others?"

Bolan saw that he had nothing left to lose. He said, "Check out a place called Oskar's. It's a gym for boxers."

"It's a pigsty," Reynek said. "Owned by the Werich syndicate. You know them?"

"Not offhand," Bolan replied.

"If we had time, I might enhance your education," Reynek told him. "But your friend needs medical attention and he needs to leave the country."

Murton's shuffling footsteps closed on Bolan from behind. "Not goin' anywhere widout my daughter," he told Reynek.

"In which case," Reynek said, "I shall be forced to place you in protective custody. You are, at the least, a material witness to multiple crimes. Perhaps you're a suspect yourself. When we find Mikoláš Zeman—"

"You won't," Murton replied, voice growing stronger, clearer by the second.

"And now, a confession of murder." Reynek shrugged at Bolan. "I'm afraid your companion leaves me no choice."

Murton came forward in a stumble-rush, growling, but Bolan intercepted him and marched him backward to the Volvo. "Stay right here and keep your mouth shut," Bolan ordered. "We might walk away from this if you don't screw it up."

"I'm here for Mandy, damn you!"

"And you blew it!" Bolan answered harshly. "Get your mind around that, will you? You're half-dead, about to be arrested, and you never came within a mile of her. If anything, you've made her situation worse."

"The hell are you talking about?" Murton challenged.

"She had value on her own," Bolan replied, voice lowered almost to a hiss. "It's hard to live with, but you know it's true. Now, thanks to you, she's turned into a fatal liability. Get it? She may be dead, thanks to your vigilante-daddy act."

The words took Murton down like body blows. His knees sagged, leaving him to clutch the Volvo for support. Bolan could hear him sobbing as he leaned in and repeated, "Right here. Mouth shut."

Back with Reynek, he asked, "So, what comes next?"

"It's getting late," the sergeant said. "If I deliver you and Mr. Murton, I'll be lucky to see home again this time tomorrow. I propose we take him to a doctor known for personal discretion, then arrange for Mr. Murton's safe return to the United States. His wealthy friends will no doubt wish to hold a grand reception."

"And me?" Bolan asked, getting to the nub of it.

Reynek lightened up a bit and said, "I hope we may be able to do business, Mr. Cooper."

WHAT ARE YOU DOING? Reynek asked himself as he drove through the early-morning streets of Prague. The stately churches of Prague's Little Quarter offered no answers in passing, for all their stained glass and pomposity. The Wallenstein Palace stood silent, devoid of advice.

Reynek did not bother checking for the Volvo's headlights in his rearview mirror. The big American would either follow him to reach the doctor's flat, or he would not. Reynek had phoned ahead, roused Dr. Vilém Koller from his badly needed beauty sleep and cautioned him to silence in the strongest terms. They understood each other, based on long acquaintance. If his luck held, there should be no leaks.

And if there were…well, Dr. Koller stood to lose the most.

His flat was situated one block south of Little Quarter Square, initially the bailey—courtyard—of Prague Castle in the thirteenth century. Later, it was the scene of public executions staged as much as entertainment for the masses as a form of legal retribution. Buildings on the square still had a vague medieval air about them, heightened by proximity to the baroque Church of Saint Nicholas.

No prayers on this night, thought Reynek as he found a parking space near Dr. Koller's old apartment house, pulled in and killed the Audi's engine. Close behind him came the Volvo, rolling past to find a slot three spaces farther down the street. Its driver exited and walked around the vehicle to help his passenger get out. Murton still had his share of trouble walking, but he managed almost unassisted until they had reached the stairs ascending to their destination on the second floor.

The doctor met them halfway, making small talk as he led his visitors upstairs, along a dingy hallway with the smell of cabbage soaked into its walls, and through the open door to his abode. Inside there, an odor of tobacco overcame the cooking smells, but Reynek also caught an undertone of disinfectant in the air.

"This way, this way," Koller instructed as he steered them toward the flat's small second bedroom, which he had converted to a makeshift operating room. His standards weren't the highest, but the lapse was understandable, since Dr. Koller's license had been stripped from him in 1995. Specific charges filed against him had included treatment of a bullet wound without reporting it to the police and peddling various prescription drugs without keeping a record of the sales.

Despite his fall from grace, Koller retained the skills that he had learned at Prague's Charles University during the seventies. Unlike some failures, though, Koller had persevered and found his niche within the underbelly of society. He was an amiable sort, particularly when intoxicated, and he seemed to blame no one but himself for his decline.

In short, a reasonable man.

"You've angered someone, I perceive," Koller told Murton as the bruised and bloodied patient stood before him. "To evaluate the damage, I must ask you to undress."

Murton disrobed without assistance. He wasn't quick about it, slumping now and then against a cabinet that held the doctor's tools, but stubbornly persisted until it was done. His naked body was a patchwork quilt of scrapes, bruises and superficial burns. It almost hurt to look at him, but Bolan had seen worse.

Much worse.

The medic peered and poked and probed, eliciting an occasional grunt of pain from Murton. He pried Murton's eyelids apart, looked into his mouth, then checked his ears and nostrils with an otoscope. When he was done, the doctor rendered judgment in a tone that was, somehow, both sympathetic and reserved at the same time.

"You have a broken nose, which I can straighten," he told Murton. "Two, perhaps three, of your ribs are cracked. I'll tape those and provide an analgesic, but they're bound to hurt for several weeks, regardless. Do not laugh, if you can possibly avoid it."

"Can't remember laughing," Murton answered.

"You have three loose teeth," Koller went on. "All molars. I am not a dentist, but you should consult one to determine if they can be saved. Your eyes are bloodshot, but they should heal if you manage to avoid a repetition of the beating. I suspect at least a mild concussion. It would be a miracle, in fact, if there was none."

"No sleep, then," Murton said.

"At least not without the proper supervision," Koller said.

"No problem," Murton said and forced a painful smile with swollen lips. "I got enough rest at the gym, when I blacked out."

"A humorist," Koller said. "That bodes well for healing. Let's begin!"

WHILE THE MEDIC WENT TO WORK on Murton, Bolan and Jan Reynek sat together in the living room. The sergeant came directly to the point.

"I take as given that you were dispatched to Prague for Mr. Murton after he was kidnapped."

"There's the girl to think about," Bolan replied.

"But you did not appear when *she* went missing, eh? Your embassy and FBI offered their full cooperation in the form of sage advice, but you are…someone else entirely."

Bolan let that go. No need to state the obvious.

"And you were *not* sent for the girl," Reynek pressed on.

"Her father's trail was fresher," Bolan said. "For all I know, the daughter's in Berlin or Damascus by now."

"The former is more likely, if she's been sold," Reynek advised. "But with the Werich syndicate—assuming, always, that she's still alive—the odds are fair to good that she remains in Prague."

"So what's the story with this Werich syndicate?"

"You aren't familiar with the operation?" Reynek seemed surprised.

"No, I'm not," Bolan admitted.

"Then your rescue of our hapless friend is all the more remarkable. Those were her men at Oskar's sty tonight and in the Citroën."

"*Her* men?"

The sergeant nodded. "Lida Werich is what you might call the 'godmother' of human trafficking in Prague. She started as an adolescent prostitute herself but had a vision of her destiny—her words—on her eighteenth birthday I've questioned her on more than one occasion. While she naturally won't admit it, that was when she killed her pimp, a scabrous Bulgar named Zlatanov, and reorganized his girls under her personal protection. It was difficult, of course, in a milieu where men had always ruled by threats and violence, but Lida dealt with them in kind. The story—unsubstantiated, or she'd be in prison now—is that she personally cut the heads off three vice lords in Prague and had them shrunken to keep as souvenirs."

"Impressive," Bolan said.

"I can confirm the murders of three major traffickers," Reynek said, "found decapitated in the city over six or eight months' time. Their heads were not recovered. Whether Lida did the job herself or hired a butcher, who can say? I wouldn't put it past her, personally."

"And it got results."

"Indeed," Reynek confirmed. "Those deaths, along with ten or fifteen lesser victims in a year of turmoil, left our Lida and her minions more or less in the catbird seat. You know that saying?"

Bolan nodded. "Yes."

"She does not run the city like a female Moriarty," Reynek said. "Please don't misunderstand me. While she has a stable of her own—most of them young, some *very* young—Lida allows her competition room to breathe and grow. All for a price, of course—like paying taxes to the government. In terms of trafficking, she supervises shipments and provides security as needed, while maintaining networks on behalf of her own brothels."

"That would be *illegal* brothels," Bolan said.

"On paper, certainly. I am the first to grant that vast corruption undermines all efforts to suppress the trade, as with drug trafficking and other kinds of contraband."

"We're talking slavery," Bolan said. "Not a load of heroin or untaxed cigarettes."

"I duly note your outrage and concur," Reynek said. "My frustration on this very point has prompted me to draft a resignation letter, which I still update from time to time and keep on my computer's hard drive."

"But you stick around."

"Perhaps I have been waiting," the sergeant said. "For an opportunity like this."

REYNEK KNEW THIN ICE when he saw it. Sitting with the big American in the quasi doctor's drab apartment, he could almost feel it cracking underneath the shabby chair he occupied.

"An opportunity for what?" the man asked.

"I think you know," Reynek replied.

"Pretend I don't, and spell it out."

Reynek resisted an impulse to sigh at Cooper's feigned ignorance. Instead, he said, "You've made a start at it tonight. I've helped, in my small way, by not arresting or reporting you. And I can do much more. *We* can achieve much more, together."

Cooper observed him for a moment, then replied, "You understand that I'm not any kind of cop. I'm not about collecting evidence for prosecutors and a jury."

"Of course! That has been tried and tried again, without success. History has convinced me that this filthy traffic cannot be suppressed by legal means."

The man frowned and said, "You can't suppress it, period. The hard truth is that there've been freaks around forever, and there always will be. Someone's going to supply whatever they desire and make a profit doing it. That's life. It won't stop. Ever."

"So, the answer is, do nothing?"

Cooper responded with a stern shake of his head. "The answer is to do what's possible, and bear in mind that next week, next month or next year you'll have to start from scratch and do it all over again."

"Understood," Reynek said. "I have no ambition to reform the human race, if such a thing were even possible. But Lida Werich is, at least in my experience, unique. Removing her and the lieutenants closest to her would, I think, be of some benefit."

"And you're all right with doing it outside the rules? Your oath of office notwithstanding?"

Reynek had debated that until it wearied him. "I am prepared to risk it," he replied.

"It's more than risk," the man cautioned him. "Go down that road, and if it doesn't kill you, then you have to *live* with it."

"I have killed men," Reynek said. He thought specifically of one rapist who had tried to slash him with a cleaver, and two bandits fleeing from a bank that they had robbed.

"I'm guessing that was self-defense. Cold blood's another proposition altogether."

"I can do it, Cooper. You will see."

"And if you're wrong, we find out in the crunch when it's too late. Maybe we both go down because you freeze."

"Would you feel better if I'd finished off those others, on the pier?" Reynek asked.

"Feeling isn't part of it," Cooper said. "Trained soldiers freeze sometimes, and others die because of it."

"So, you're afraid I'll get you killed?" Reynek could not suppress a smile.

"Survival's high on my list of priorities. And it should be high on yours, unless you're crazy."

"I assure you, I am not."

"So bottom-line it for me, Reynek. You're prepared to break the law, including murder, as a means of taking down this network?"

"Absolutně," Reynek answered. "Yes. I absolutely am."

"And you won't have any trouble snowing your superiors?"

"Snowing?"

"Avoiding. Ducking. Lying to them while you run around the city tearing up their rule book."

"They allow me a fair measure of autonomy," Reynek said. "I was flattered for a time, until I understood that they expected me to fail."

"So, part of this is settling with the brass," the man beside him said.

"They would obstruct me if they understood my plan," Reynek said. "That would be...unfortunate."

"I don't shoot cops. No matter what."

Reynek processed that information. Nodded. "There are some whom I would happily dispose of," he replied. "If we should meet them...well, leave them to me."

Frowning, the big American said, "Okay. Tell me more about this godmother of yours."

HALF AN HOUR LATER, Murton joined them in the living room with Dr. Koller on his heels, ready to catch the patient if he took a spill. It wasn't necessary, as the former SEAL was fairly steady on his feet, albeit stiff and clearly feeling pain from the results of his ordeal. His broken nose was taped and splinted, which might serve as a disguise when he left Prague, with blackened eyes above the tape and swollen lips below. The rest of Murton's injuries and bandages, including the elastic binding on his rib cage, were concealed beneath his clothing. Bolan watched him settle slowly on a chair, well to the front and grimacing.

"All right," Murton said. "What's the plan?"

"We put you on the next flight headed stateside," Bolan said.

If Murton flushed with anger, it was hidden by his bruises. "Leave without my daughter? Not a chance in hell!"

"You took your shot," Bolan replied, "and this is where it got you. If you'd managed to survive another day, it would have been a miracle. Like I said before, as for your daughter, she was better off before you came to Prague. Your clumsy blitz turned that around, made her a liability."

"You're wrong!" Murton said. "I'm no idiot. You think I told the pricks I talked to who I am? You think I mentioned Mandy's name, for God's sake?"

"Think about it," Bolan answered back. "They snatch a girl from California. Two days later, a man from California shows up grilling pimps all over Prague. You may not be an idiot, but neither are the people you've been hunting. They were smart enough to bag you, anyway."

"What are you saying, then?" Murton demanded. "Would they... Do you think they've... Jesus Christ! You think *I* killed my little girl?"

"No one has said that," Reynek interjected. "There is nothing to support it." He was sensitive enough to leave the *yet* unspoken.

"What I'm saying," Bolan told the grieving father, "is that you increased her risk through careless action. Can we find her once you've moved out of the way? I couldn't say. But every minute wasted sitting here, debating it with you, thins out the odds."

"I *can't* go home without her," Murton answered through clenched teeth. "Suppose she was your daughter. What would you do?"

Bolan's only repsonse was cold silence.

"Listen," Murton said. "I've been trained for this. I'm a professional."

"*Were* a professional," Bolan replied. "You've been behind a desk too long."

"All right. I messed up. Don't you think I know it? But—"

"And now you're nearly crippled," Bolan interrupted. "What are we supposed to do, wheel you around and use you for a human shield?"

"Goddamn you!"

"End of argument," Bolan said. "You'll be on the next flight out that has a seat available. Put up a fight, and Dr. Koller can sedate you for the first leg of the trip, with someone from the embassy to babysit."

"You dirty bastards!"

"This is a battle," Bolan told him, "not an ego trip."

His brutal words had the desired effect. With something like a sob, Murton nodded and lowered his head as he replied, "All right. Okay. You win."

"You have an alternate ID that you can use for traveling?" Bolan asked.

"Back at my hotel. The Mamaison."

"We'll pick it up on our way to the airport," Bolan said. "Along with your bags."

"I'm entrusting my daughter to you," Murton told him. "If you let me down—"

More cruel truth was required.

"She's been gone for six days," Bolan said. "I've already told you that we may not find her. If you're looking for a scapegoat, pick somebody else."

A muttered curse from Murton, but he nodded, shoulders slumping. Bolan caught Jan Reynek watching him, a frown etched on his face.

"What?" he inquired.

The sergeant shook his head. "Nothing."

"You want to play in my world," Bolan told him, "this is how it starts."

5

Lida Werich sipped a glass of Becherovka, savoring the taste of cinnamon and anise on her tongue before the alcohol kicked in. Some Czechs believed the herbal bitters helped digestion, and she hoped they were correct, because her stomach churned with anger and a faint tinge of anxiety.

Werich was five feet seven inches tall, one hundred forty well-proportioned pounds distributed over her frame in such a way that men who'd never met her still looked twice—and sometimes more—in passing on the street. Her hair, once mousy brown, was now strawberry blond, thanks to religious application of the proper chemicals. Werich did not waste time in hair salons, of course; Prague's leading stylist came to her, upon demand. At forty, she could pass for ten years younger on a good day.

But this day, barely three hours old, had already gone bad.

"Tell me again," she ordered after she had drained her glass. "You, this time."

Her green eyes focused like gun barrels on one of the two men who stood before her desk. He was the taller of the pair, disheveled hair adding a little to his height in compensation for slumped shoulders. Neither man looked happy to be facing Werich in her private office, neither of them seemingly grateful that they had escaped a recent brush with death.

"I don't know what to say," Zdeněk Vojan replied, his voice almost a whisper.

Werich gave him one of her beguiling smiles and said, "Tell me your version of what happened. What went wrong tonight?"

"Um…well…as Michal said, the four of us drove out to Oskar's. It was change of shift, you know, for watching the American."

"Interrogating him," Werich corrected.

"*Prosim,* madam. He is…he was…a tough one."

"So, you drove to the gymnasium…"

"And when we got out of the car, we saw the prisoner outside, walking away. Another man was with him, helping him along."

"And you pursued them?"

"*Prosim*…well, first thing, we got back in the car."

"Instead of chasing them on foot?"

"Jiří demanded it," Vojan said. "They were almost to the corner, and he thought they might outrun us otherwise."

"One man dragging another who was injured? Outrun four of you?"

The man shrugged. "I'm paid to follow orders, madam, not to think about them."

"Just as well." Werich sneered, making Vojan cringe. "What happened then?"

"We all got in the car and followed, but they reached another car before we overtook them. It's a blur to me from that point, madam. Jiří shouting orders at Ivan and firing his pistol, the second car coming from nowhere—"

"Ah, yes. Tell me more about this second car," Werich commanded.

"Well, madam…I only saw its headlights coming up behind us," Vojan said. The sour odor of the man's fear and sweat made Werich's nose twitch. "First, we thought they were police, but there were no sirens or flashers."

"They? You're saying *they?* How many were there in the second car?"

Vojan glanced over toward his fellow failure, Michal Lobkovic, as if hoping to find the answer written on his face. "I don't…madam…it's just a turn of phrase. I never had a view inside the other car. Just headlights, blinding me."

Useless, she thought, but told him, "All right. Go ahead."

"Yes, madam. Um…they led us to the waterfront, I cannot say exactly where."

"Let us assume it's the location where police retrieved your car," Werich suggested.

"Right. The car we were pursuing—it was some kind of Volvo—turned around in front of us before we knew it, and the driver started shooting. He hit Ivan, at the wheel, and then we crashed. I struck my head—" a shaky hand rose toward his matted scalp for confirmation "—and lost consciousness. I came around in time to rouse Michal and get away before the *policie* arrived."

"How fortunate for both of you," Werich said. "And while you were sleeping, you saw nothing of the second car? You can't say what became of the American?"

Their two heads shook in unison. Vojan said, "No, madam."

"Because you were unconscious."

Both men nodded.

"Perhaps that is a state you should maintain," Werich suggested as she raised a silencer-equipped CZ 100 pistol from her lap and drilled Vojan's left eye with a 9 mm Parabellum round.

He dropped without a whimper to the onyx floor, which was impervious to blood. Before his friend could speak or move, she had him covered, with the muzzle of her weapon centered on his heaving chest.

"The only reason that I don't flay you for lamp shades," she informed him, "is because I want you to go out and spread the word. Tell everyone you know *exactly* what becomes of men who disappoint me."

"Yes, madam! I will! Thank you, madam!"

She reconsidered, muttered *"kurva"* to herself and shot him through the heart. Already feeling better, Werich set the gun aside, stood and, addressing the latest corpse, said, "On second thought, don't bother. I'll tell them myself."

BOOKING A FLIGHT for Andrew Murton proved less difficult than Bolan had expected, thanks in large part to Jan Reynek's PCR credentials. After driving Murton to the Mamaison on Belgicka Street, where they retrieved his bags and two sets of alternate ID, they'd taken him to Prague Ruzyně International and shopped around for flights leaving the Czech Republic. Reynek booked him on the first plane heading out to Paris, with connecting flights from Charles de Gaulle to London Heathrow, and from there to JFK. A call to Brognola by sat-phone guaranteed that G-men would be waiting on the ground, stateside, to debrief Murton on arrival.

Murton's bruised and bandaged mien wasn't a great match for the photo in a passport that proclaimed him to be Alexander Moss from San Franciso, but Jan Reynek managed to persuade airport security that "Moss" had been the victim of a hit-and-run in Prague's Old Town, barely escaping death while on his way to visit the Golz-Kinský Palace. Bolan thought they could have done without specifics, but the sergeant sold it, gladhanding the other uniforms as members of a close fraternity.

They stayed with Murton through the boarding call, then waited until he was in the air before they left the terminal. Whatever happened to the grieving, tortured dad from that point on, at least he would not be in Bolan's line of fire.

And fire was coming. There could be no doubt of that.

They'd driven Reynek's Audi to the airport, Bolan taking it on faith that the excursion wouldn't prove to be a trap. The Volvo waited for them back at Reynek's place in New Town, where they'd stopped to leave it on their way to the Mamaison from Dr. Koller's covert clinic. Upon arrival, Bolan checked his stash of arms, then left them in the car and followed Reynek up a flight of outdoor stairs to the man's apartment.

Yet another possibilty for ambush, but it didn't happen. Bolan had begun to trust the Czech policeman—to a point, at least.

He hadn't seen Reynek in action yet and only had the sergeant's word that he could pull a trigger when it mattered, even if the target had his back turned and was unaware of death advancing on him from behind. If Reynek proved to be a squeamish soldier, let his scruples get the better of him, he would not last long in Bolan's down-and-dirty world.

Inside Reynek's flat, with dawn breaking outside, Bolan passed on an offer of vodka and settled for coffee. They sat at a small kitchen table, Formica and tubular steel. There was no trace of a female influence in sight. Reynek sat facing him, seemed relaxed as he said, "This game, as you call it, is all new to me. How should we begin?"

"It's already begun," Bolan said. "We've deprived them of something they wanted. They're bound to resent it, take punitive steps. Are you clear, as to family, if you're identified?"

Reynek considered the question, then nodded. "There's no one," he answered. "Oh, cousins in Zlín and Karviná, but they wouldn't know me from Adam. I haven't seen any of them since I got out of short pants."

"Close friends?" Bolan pressed him.

A head shake. "Colleagues," Reynek said, "but we don't socialize. I'm excluded for failure to…how is it said in your country? To go with the flow?"

"That's the phrase," Bolan said. "Once we're rolling, you think they'll suspect you?"

"Of breaking the rules?" Reynek smiled. "Not a chance."

"Fair enough. All we need now are targets. I normally start at the bottom and work my way up, if there's time."

"And is there?"

"Depends if we're trying to locate the girl."

"A lost cause, I suppose." Reynek didn't sound positive.

"Still, it could be worth a try. Shake the tree," Bolan said. "See what drops."

"By all means, then," the sergeant replied. "Let the shaking begin."

VLADIMIR NEFF EXPERIENCED uncustomary nervousness as he approached the Ministry of Justice on Vyšehradská Street, in Prague's New Town. It was not morning traffic that distressed him, since he did not drive himself to work. As deputy minister of justice for the Czech Republic, Neff was entitled to limousine service and took full advantage of the privilege, riding in comfort with a bodyguard who—in his personal opinion, though never voiced aloud—was more or less superfluous.

Nor was the trouble on his mind a matter of security. At forty-eight years old, Neff was within close grasping distance of the highest office he could reasonably hope to occupy. His round and often sour face was not constructed with a televised career in mind, and he had long ago admitted to himself that he could never be prime minister or president. Neither his aspect nor his temperament were suited to a role as head of state or chief of parliament. But Neff believed he *could* aspire to be the minister of justice, and, in fact, his quiet campaign to secure that post was well advanced.

Of course, that effort could be easily derailed. A scandal, if it stuck, would scuttle any hopes Neff had of further personal advancement and might even put him on the street without a job. He wouldn't starve—Neff had too many wealthy friends, and too much money stashed in secret bank accounts for that to happen—but the damage to his ego would be crippling. After decades of establishing and polishing his image, just the thought of the threat of cracks in the facade produced a spill of acid in his stomach and a painful throbbing in his skull.

The latest, not-so-subtle threat had come from Lida Werich. She had called Neff at his home, as usual, avoiding any traceable connection to the ministry itself, and burdened him with updates on the situation with their rogue American in Prague. The conversation put Neff off his breakfast, and the coffee he had drunk while on the telephone was burbling like molten lava in his gut.

Their problem had been bad enough when Andrew Murton turned up on his own, seeking the daughter whom he claimed had been abducted from the Hotel Rott on Little Square. Neff had already known about the case, from briefings by the PCR and FBI, and had been assured in fact that all possible steps were being taken to retrieve the girl or find her corpse. Neff understood why Murton would be less than satisfied with that report, but when the man had run amok he violated every rule of protocol, committing half a dozen felonies. His actions made the government—and more specifically, the Ministry of Justice—seem incompetent.

In truth, Neff was relieved when Murton disappeared, presumably eliminated by the very traffickers he had accused of kidnapping his daughter. There was "heat," of course, as the Americans would say, but Neff went through the motions: posting a reward for information leading to the vanished man's recovery or any leads pertaining to his daughter; questioning individuals who might know something of the matter but, in fact, did not; increasing security surrounding any other tours by foreign students passing through the capital and countryside.

All smoke and mirrors, while he waited for the natural excitement to subside.

But then, this mess.

Not only was Murton still alive, but he had managed to escape from Werich's clutches, aided by an unidentified armed man who left raw carnage in his wake. Five men were dead, according to police reports—seven by Werich's count, which Neff preferred not to examine closely—and the rogue American had vanished once again. He might be plotting further depredations at this very moment, prepared to spring from hiding and wreak havoc on the streets.

Werich required help bringing him to heel, and she had called on Neff.

And if he failed her, what might the woman do? What might she whisper to the media or to a prosecutor that would bring Neff's whole world crashing down around his ears?

Don't fail, then, he advised himself. *Above all, do not fail.*

JAKUB GROSSMANN was considering which robe to wear that morning when his secretary interrupted him. The choice was hardly taxing, since the robes were all identical, jet-black, befitting a Superior Court judge, but Grossmann still frowned at the interruption.

"Yes? What is it?" he demanded.

Stella Krejcar, Grossmann's private secretary since his first appointment to the bench as a district judge in Rakovník, all of twenty years ago, took no offense at his brusque attitude. Expressionless, she said, "You have a call, sir. Deputy Minister Neff on line two."

Grossmann frowned at the mention of Neff, who never called except to beg a favor. "Very well," he answered, adding "thank you" as a tardy afterthought.

Alone once more, Grossmann crossed his chambers to the large teak desk that filled a quarter of the room. Reluctantly, he raised the telephone receiver to his ear and pressed the lighted button for the line in use.

"Deputy Minister!" he gushed, adept at counterfeit enthusiasm when it was required. "How may I help you?"

Without apology for the disturbance, Neff launched straight into his spiel. "You are familiar with the Murton business, I believe?"

I should be, Grossmann thought, *since you informed me of it personally.* But he simply said, "I am."

"Unfortunately, there has been a new development. A complication, I should say."

Guessing, Grossmann replied, "The child has been discovered?"

"No, no. It's the *father.* We now have information that his disappearance was a staged event, a publicity stunt as it were. He resurfaced last night, with an accomplice, and it seems they've murdered several men whom Murton blamed for the abduction of his daughter."

"Are you certain that it's him?"

"The PCR has witnesses," Neff said. "As for the second man, he has not been identified so far."

"Incredible!"

And to be sure, it has the rank smell of fresh hovno *about it,* the judge thought.

"There's no doubt, I assure you," Neff said. "One might say he's demented from grief, but his actions cannot be excused or ignored. And his companion...well, it smacks of a conspiracy."

"By whom?" Grossmann asked.

"Who can say? It's known that Murton was a covert fighting man, what the *Američané* call a 'Navy SEAL.' No doubt, he still has friends in that line, perhaps clandestine mercenaries."

Stranger by the moment, Grossmann thought. "I must ask what this has to do with me."

"It's vital that we find these men and stop them before they wreak any further havoc in the city," Neff replied.

"Of course," Grossmann agreed. "But if you've mobilized the PCR—"

"I need emergency arrest warrants," Neff interrupted. "One for Andrew Murton and the other for 'Jan Novák.'"

"Ah." The Czech equivalent of tried-and-true "John Doe." Grossmann asked Neff, "And you are seeking to avoid the normal offering of evidence, I take it?"

"As I said," Neff answered, stiffly, "this is an *emergency*. These felons pose a danger to the public order and to every citizen of Prague."

Assuming every citizen of Prague worked for a certain Lida Werich, Grossmann thought, but dared not voice the observation. Caving in, he said, "I understand, Deputy Minister. My clerk will have the standard forms prepared immediately."

"Excellent. I shall await the courier," Neff said. "Your prompt cooperation will not be forgotten."

As the line went dead, Grossmann was left to wonder if that parting comment was a thank-you or a threat, thinly disguised.

A SECOND POT OF COFFEE led to breakfast—called *snídane* by the locals—featuring fried eggs, some kind of pastry topped with poppy seeds, plum jam and yogurt on the side. Bolan and Reynek finished off their list of targets as they ate, focused on Prague primarily, but tossing in a few sites farther afield in case the city got too hot and they required some breathing room.

"To intercept the foreign shipments is impossible without specific information as to time and place," Reynek explained. "You understand that children and women arrive from so many countries. I myself have known victims imported from Slovakia, Bulgaria, Belarus, Russia, Lithuania, Romania, Moldova and Ukraine. More recently, we have reports of shipments from the Far East, seen as more exotic by a jaded clientele. How many thousands cross our borders in a given year, and how many remain, nobody knows."

"I take it that the border checkpoints aren't too rigorous," Bolan said.

"In the old days, under communism, certainly," Reynek replied. "But since we joined the *Evropská unie*—the European Union—not so much. The Schengen Agreement abolished passport controls for most of the present EU in 1985, to ensure what our politicians call free movement of persons, products and capital."

"Unless I missed the memo," Bolan said, "all EU member states also have laws in place to punish human trafficking."

"Oh, certainly." Jan Reynek fanned the air between them with a hand, as if dispersing pesky gnats. "The laws exist and are enforced as the police and courts see fit. A scandal may arise from time to time, as with the Murton child, but they all pass. Business returns to normal. If the victim, as in this case, is not found…well, who's to say she was not taken by some random pedophile? Or possibly, she fell into the Vltava and drowned, her body swept away downstream. Perhaps a wels catfish has made a meal of her by now."

"We know what happened to the girl," Bolan replied.

"But *knowing* is not *proof,* my friend. To rouse the vast, complacent public, you must have a victim who is visible *and* sympathetic. Do not bother them with some worn-out *děvka* who has worked in every brothel from Kiev to Rome and back. They don't care about addicts who have thrown their lives away and now receive what most good Christian folk believe they probably deserve. Show them a child snatched from the bosom of her family, and yes! You have their full attention for a day, a week, perhaps even a month. Beyond that, *pfft!* There'll always be another fascinating crisis coming off the assembly line."

Bolan devoutly wished that he could disagree, but everything the sergeant said was true. No matter where you went on earth, police and politicians had their hands out, while the media devoured everyone in sight and spat them out again. Corruption was the rule in politics, some jurisdictions worse than others, and the great "silent majority" was stirred to outrage only intermittently, halfheartedly, by some specific tragedy. On balance—in the States, at least—he'd found more anger focused on publicized philanderings of statesmen than the daily brutal shame inflicted on so many helpless victims nationwide.

"So, if we really want to raise some hell," he said, "we need to find the girl."

A nod from Reynek. "Certainly, it would be to our benefit. And hers as well, of course."

"And failing that," Bolan went on, "we make this Lida Werich and her playmates wish we'd found her."

"Very good," Reynek said.

"What's your routine like at work?" Bolan asked. "How soon will they miss you, if you don't show up?"

"I can report by telephone unless they summon me," Reynek answered. "To say that anyone would miss me is, I think, a gross exaggeration."

"So we're good to go on the street," Bolan said. "Working up from the bottom?"

"Dekonce malé ryby jsou ryby," Reynek said.

"I didn't catch that."

"It means 'Even small fish are fish.' Let us go cast the hook."

6

The flight from Prague to Paris was a short one, just over an hour in the air. Resisting the fatigue that sent his thoughts roaming astray and beckoned him to sleep, Andrew Murton drank coffee and stayed wide awake, planning what he would do upon arrival.

First thing: watch for FBI agents or embassy staffers who might have been called out to meet him and make sure he boarded his flight to New York. Since that trip was not part of his plan, going home without Mandy a failure he couldn't abide, he would have to avoid them if any were waiting to greet him.

To that end, he visited the Boeing 727's lavatory fifteen minutes prior to landing, standing slumped inside the cubicle that made a phone booth seem expansive, studying the ruin of his face in a mirror cast from polished stainless steel. The nasal splint would have to go, along with the adhesive tape, so Murton clinched his aching teeth and went to work, swallowing low, involuntary moans of pain. He couldn't hide the shiners without makeup, which was unavailable, but careful re-arrangement of his hair partly concealed the butterfly bandage securing a cut at his hairline. The result was an improvement, though he wouldn't pass a close inspection, most particularly if a team of escorts had his photograph in hand.

Something to think about when he was on the ground. But for the moment, a hasty survey showed him that his other inju-

ries were hidden and would not be readily apparent if he sucked
it up, ignored the pain that rippled through his body every time
he made a move. Walk tall and straight, without a hitch, and
maybe he could pull it off.

Unless he had to fight.

The outcome, in that case, would depend on numbers, size
and skill. Murton wasn't concerned about some paper pusher
from the embassy, but if the FBI sent people out, they would
be armed and reasonably skilled in self-defense. A ruckus in
the terminal at Charles de Gaulle would jeopardize his hopes
of getting back to Prague. Even if he could dodge a setup at
the airport, flying would be out, which meant he'd have to
find a car somehow—no money in his pocket but the pit-
tance he'd been given by his rescuers for in-flight meals—
and navigate six hundred miles or so across three countries
to his destination. Make that four, unless he circumvented
tiny Luxembourg.

It would be difficult but not impossible. Far better if he could
avoid a hassle at the terminal, trade in his tickets to New York
and find a seat aboard the next flight headed back to Prague.

Murton had never been religious, but he said a quick prayer.
For Mandy's sake. He wasn't sure exactly what to pray for,
hardly dared to ask that he would find his daughter safe and
sound after the best part of a week in savage hands. To simply find her *living,* maybe…or would that be cursing her to
bear the scars inflicted on her flesh and memory while in
captivity?

Should he be praying for her swift release from suffering,
instead?

And did it matter, finally, if there was no one listening?

Murton had eavesdropped on his rescuers, discovered that
they had some plan in mind to hassle Werich and her minions.
Fine. He wished them well and was supremely grateful that
they'd saved his life. But sitting out the rest of it while others
did his fighting for him, with his daughter's life at stake, was
more than he could bear.

And if his own plan interfered with theirs, well, that was too damned bad.

It was a rule of thumb for airliners to keep their cabin temperature on the chilly side. On other flights, with only cash and contracts hanging in the balance, Murton often closed the air vents overhead to spare himself a cold. Today, he twisted them wide open to offset the steady throbbing in his skull.

There was no danger of a chill this morning, on the flight to Charles de Gaulle.

Murton had boundless, seething hate to keep him warm.

SEX TOURISM OPERATES like any other business, with controllers and administrators at the top, in charge of regulating the supply to meet demand. Below the CEOs and CFOs are the procurers and suppliers, lawyers to defend them if they run afoul of honest cops and wranglers who control the stables, often with the aid of one or more professional enforcers. Victims seduced, shanghaied or dragged by force into the service of a prostitution syndicate are chattel, the equivalent of slaves on a plantation that produces nothing but a steady flow of cash for those atop the pyramid of misery.

And then, there are the customers.

Whether their taste is male or female, young or old, they come from every race, religion, nationality and walk of life. Doctors and lawyers, ministers and teachers, rock-and-roll celebrities with cash to burn, and hard-hat laborers who had to scrimp and save for an excursion to the dark side. Nearly all cherish illusions that their mental twist is "normal," although sadly out of favor at the moment. They survive and stay at liberty by keeping up facades.

Sex traffickers cater to those illusions, playing along for the good of their business. Advertising on the internet and in selected publications usually skirted the legal issues. They speak in euphemisms and leave photos to communicate the message. Upon arrival at their chosen destination, customers are seldom driven from the airport to a brothel for a hasty hit-and-run.

In Prague, one pit stop on a pervo-tourist's journey to the sewer was a New Town nightclub called Opustit—translated by Jan Reynek to mean "Abandon." It was closed at half past eight o'clock, its denizens banished by daylight to their jobs or hidey-holes, but Bolan hadn't picked the place to score a body count. He meant to send a message, starting at the bottom.

And it didn't get much lower than Opustit.

Reynek had described the club while they were driving over. It was operated by a thug named Radola Bubeníček, who ran the operation on behalf of Werich. Outwardly, Opustit was a bar for swinging singles. Underneath the half-assed glitter, it facilitated meetings between pedophiles and pimps, while Bubeníček maintained a thriving drug trade on the side.

Bolan and Reynek went in through the back door, crudely jimmied with a crowbar Reynek brought along to serve in place of keys. Though no alarm was audible, Reynek had cased the joint beforehand and had described to Bolan its silent system, which would summon both police and some of Werich's personal security brigade.

No time to waste.

Before embarking on their raid, Bolan and Reynek had emptied a dozen plastic bottles of Mattoni Sport mineral water, then refilled them with a mix of gasoline and powdered laundry detergent, producing a crude but effective version of napalm. Each had a wick attached, moistened with gasoline to complete the Molotov cocktail. Once inside the club, they separated quickly and went to work, Bolan operating from his memory of Reynek's hand-drawn floor plan.

"Ten minutes tops," Reynek had said. "Then, we have to deal with the police." Speaking as if he wasn't one of them—which might be true on this day, on more levels than Reynek even understood.

Instead of tossing the cocktails, Bolan placed them in preselected locations—one on Bubeníček's desk, for a personal touch—before sparking their wicks with a cheap disposable lighter. The plastic bottles wouldn't shatter if he threw them, anyway, but Bolan knew the burning wicks would melt holes large enough to ignite the jellied contents and produce a blaze impervious to water.

Cleansing fire.

The club was probably insured, but Bolan wasn't angling for a major shot at Werich's wallet. Not yet, anyway. Torching Opustit was a shot across her bow, to let the queen bee of the scumbags know that her problems hadn't gone away when Murton caught his flight to JFK.

In fact, they were only beginning.

Bolan and Reynek were back in the Volvo and rolling before smoke began to seep out of Opustit through gaps around windows and doors. By the time the first Škoda Octavia squad car arrived on the scene, the nightclub was already beyond earthly help. Unknown to the responding officers, a fire sale was in progress.

And everything must go.

CAPTAIN KAREL TUREK, of the PCR's Agency for Particular Activities of Criminal Police, left his car and driver in the Ministry of Justice parking lot and entered through a door tagged *Pro Úředníky Pouze*—For Officials Only. Rank had privileges, one of the least among them being leave to pass where no civilian was allowed to go.

Turek was not in uniform. His unit of the PCR was an investigative branch, with the "particular activities" vaguely defined to give its officers the widest latitude available. While other branches of the PCR dealt with financial crimes, narcotics, protection of public officials and atrocities committed by the Czech Republic's former communist regime, the APACP's responsibilities ranged from pursuit of terrorists to oversight of Czech police themselves, a sort of Internal Affairs for the nation at large. It was a catchall kind of duty, and its many opportunities for personal enrichment pleased Captain Turek to no end.

The same could not be said for this morning's appointment with Deputy Minister of Justice Vladimir Neff. Turek regarded Neff with high disdain as a pathetic sycophant but kept that opinion to himself with a survivor's instinct for the nuances of bureaucratic gamesmanship. Neff would be gone one day, replaced by yet another suit unqualified to speak on any aspect of police work, while Turek and others like him bore the weight of keeping order in society.

Neff's summons had been curt, peremptory. He sounded worried on the telephone, a first impression buttressed when he failed to keep Turek waiting for the usual fifteen minutes under scrutiny from Neff's bleached-blonde receptionist. Instead, she ushered him directly in to meet the Great One in his inner sanctum, planted as he always was behind a desk the size of a billiards table.

"Captain, sit!" No *please* attached to it, of course, as Neff waved Turek toward a waiting chair.

"Deputy Minister, good morning."

"Hardly," Neff replied, tight-lipped. "You've heard the latest news, I take it?"

"News concerning…?"

"Andrew Murton? And the fire?"

"Perhaps a bit more detail…"

"Murton! The American whose daughter—"

"I'm aware of who he is, sir. As of last report, he had gone missing here in Prague."

"That's old news, Captain," Neff informed him. "Murton surfaced once again, early this morning, with a male accomplice unidentified so far. They've murdered several men, presumably suspected by this crazed American in the abduction of his daughter, and within the past half hour may have burned a nightclub in New Town."

"May have?" Turek was stalling while he processed Neff's report.

"The club—it's called Opustit, or at least it *was*—reportedly has some connection to red-light activities. You follow me?"

"Yes, sir. And this supposed connection, you presume, is Murton's motive for destroying it?"

"What else?"

"The milieu you describe is not without its petty feuds, Deputy Minister. One pimp regards another as trespassing on his territory, maybe poaching *šlapky* from his stable, and decides to teach an object lesson."

Neff frowned and asked, "Do you believe the timing of these incidents is mere coincidence?"

Turek allowed himself a shrug. "Without investigating, sir, I couldn't say."

"Precisely! It's for that reason exactly that I've called you, Captain. I wish you to mount a full investigation—quietly, of course, there's no need to alert the media—and find this damned American before he wreaks more havoc in our city."

"If, in fact, he is responsible," Turek replied.

"In any case," Neff countered, "for the murder charge alone, a warrant has been issued for the arrest of Andrew Murton and his cohort, known for the time being as 'Jan Novák.'"

Stifling an urge to scowl, Turek said, "As you wish, Deputy Minister."

"Report to me directly, yes? Keep this between the two of us, for now."

"Yes, sir."

"Good man. Dismissed!"

Mouthing a silent curse when he had turned his back on Neff, the captain marched out with the bearing of the soldier he had been, before he joined the PCR and pledged his honor to enforcement of the law. While there was precious little of his honor left, he still preserved the image of a lawman. And as such, he naturally cultivated contacts on the wrong side of the law.

A starting place of sorts, from which to seek a rogue American and his accomplice, still unknown. Perhaps a means of running them to earth and stopping them, before they wreaked more havoc on the city's seamy underground.

TORCHING OPUSTIT HAD BEEN Reynek's test run, starting with an easy mark, but Bolan still wasn't convinced the police officer could go the distance in this kind of war. He hadn't seen the sergeant pull a trigger yet, and lighting up an empty club was child's play in the final scheme of things. Next up, Bolan required a target where they'd meet some opposition. Nothing heavy, necessarily, but adequate to see how Reynek did when he was under fire instead of simply setting one.

Which brought them to a stately home off Dlouha Street, a block beyond the southeastern border of Prague's historic Jewish Quarter. It could have been the mansion of a wealthy merchant dynasty—and may have been exactly that, in days gone by—but presently it housed a different kind of family. A matriarchy, you might say, with one den mother and at least two dozen women occupying rooms at any given time.

Plus the security, of course.

Bolan had picked an adult brothel as their second mark because he didn't want a flock of panicked children on his hands if Reynek dropped the ball. From this point on he'd have a better feel for Reynek's capabilities, and they could strike deeper into the Werich syndicate's domain.

If Reynek pulled his weight, that is.

And if both of them survived.

They motored past the Church of Saint Castulus, then turned left, away from the ancient Jewish Quarter, with Reynek directing Bolan toward their target. It stood out, even in a neighborhood of houses that were oversize, reeking of history and money. If he'd had the time to daydream, Bolan might have pictured horse-drawn carriages moving along the streets, liveried drivers wearing wigs that made them all look like George Washington.

But not on this day.

The mansion had a mossy wall and pillars for a gate out front, but no actual gate in evidence. Bolan pulled in, powered the Volvo to a turnaround that placed them near the tall front doors and watched the windows as he asked Reynek, "You ready?"

"Yes."

Reynek had brought along a CZW 9PS submachine gun that he carried in his car, chambered in 9×19 mm Parabellum. It measured sixteen inches overall, with folded stock, and claimed a cyclic rate of seven hundred fifty rounds per minute in full-auto mode. Its fire-selector switch also allowed for three-round bursts and semiauto fire. A decent weapon, Bolan thought, in the right hands.

That was the part he was about to test.

He took the Vz. 58V with him, just in case, and climbed six granite steps to reach the mansion's wide veranda. The doorbell was a sterling-silver antique with a dangling chain. It produced a burring sound inside the house when Bolan tugged the chain, then stepped back to await whatever happened next.

He was about to try again, after a full two minutes, when the door opened on well-oiled hinges to reveal the lady of the house. Well, one of them, at least. The madam saw them standing on her threshold, both at ease with arms behind their backs, and said something in Czech that Bolan didn't understand.

"Anglicky prosím," Reynek answered.

"English? Of course," the madam said. "How may I help you?"

"We're the renovators," Bolan said.

"I'm sorry? Reno—"

"Stavební dělníci," Reynek interrupted.

"You do not look like workmen," she replied. "And I'm afraid you are mistaken, gentlemen. We have no plans for new construction on the house."

"We're more into the demolition side," Bolan said as he brought his rifle into view.

She bolted, risked a bullet in the back if they were hitters, shouting out what sounded like a name. Bolan made no move to restrain her, entering the house with Reynek on his heels and waiting for the muscle to appear.

They came from different rooms downstairs, one in his undershirt, both clutching pistols. "Yours," Bolan said with a nod off to his right, and met the other with a short burst from his carbine that eliminated any threat from that quarter.

Beside him, Reynek fired a burst of six or seven rounds that dropped the second shooter in his tracks. If it affected him at all, no evidence of any inner turmoil showed up on his face.

"Okay," Bolan said, feeling more at ease with his new ally. "Let's clean house."

IT TURNED OUT that the embassy had sent one man, apparently unarmed, to greet Murton at Charles de Gaulle and shepherd him to his connecting flight. The minor diplomat took one look at his battered face and winced.

"They said you'd had an accident, but—"

"I'm all right," Murton cut in. "You drew the short straw for the babysitting detail?"

"More or less," the flunky answered, almost blushing. "Jack Pierce, assistant to the deputy attaché for—"

"I'd like to hit the head before we share life stories," Murton interrupted him.

"The head? Oh, right. The lav," Pierce translated from Navy-speak. "It's on the way down to your gate. Cutting it close, with twenty minutes till you board."

"I won't be long," Murton assured him.

"Okay, then."

They moved on from the Czech Airlines arrival gate through Terminal 2D, angling toward the nearest public restrooms before proceeding to Murton's Air France connection to JFK, in nearby Terminal 2E. Pierce jabbered on as if he felt compelled to make small talk, avoiding any further mention of the trouble Murton had experienced in Prague. He didn't mention Mandy, either, making Murton wonder whether he was trying to be tactful or whether the man's boss had skipped the details in his briefing.

Either way, it made no difference.

As long as Pierce was with him, Murton could not execute

his plan. Elimination of the watchdog was his first priority, and he would have to handle it in such a manner as to buy himself some time.

Because he was not flying to New York in twenty minutes. Not a snowball's chance.

The best way to ensure his lead time was to kill Pierce and conceal his body well enough that no one would discover it for several hours, but he balked at murdering a hapless gofer from the embassy for personal convenience. Instead, he'd have to incapacitate his escort and secure Pierce so that when he regained consciousness, he would be gagged and bound, delayed substantially from sounding an alarm.

Inside the restroom, Murton feigned a stomach cramp that let him dip his head and peer beneath the half doors of the nearby toilet stalls. All empty. He timed his next move as Pierce stepped forward, visibly concerned and trying to assist him.

"Hey, are you—"

Stiff fingers caught Pierce in the solar plexus, driving all the air out of his lungs. Murton stopped short of killing force and caught Pierce as he fell, looped one arm tight around his babysitter's neck and put the lights out by constricting his carotid arteries. Pierce slumped in Murton's grip, the dead weight lancing pain through Murton's ribs as he dragged the man across the restroom, to the last stall in the lineup.

He chose the handicapped stall for its extra floor space, shut and latched the door behind him, then turned his full attention to the limp form at his feet. He stripped off Pierce's belt and used it to secure the man's limp arms behind his back. A handkerchief from Pierce's pocket filled his mouth, while Murton tied his own around the downed man's head to keep the gag in place. Last but not least, he used the escort's shoelaces to bind his ankles, then wedged Pierce into a corner near the toilet, out of sight from anyone who passed the stall.

That done, he stood and listened, verified that no one had walked in while he was binding Pierce. Leaving the stall latched from inside would further stall discovery of Pierce, but Murton wasn't sure his ribs would let him climb over the steel partition separating his stall from the next. Instead, he crouched, then lay down on the tile floor and wriggled out beneath the door.

So far, so good.

He had ID, a valid credit card and—hopefully—sufficient time to book and board another flight.

Unfinished business waited for him, back in Prague.

7

Suburban Přední Kopanina is located six miles northwest of Prague's city center. Its outstanding features include Prague Ruzyně International Airport and a nine-hundred-year-old Romanesque rotunda dedicated to St. Mary Magdalene. Neither attraction had drawn Bolan and Reynek to the neighborhood at half past nine on the first morning of their war against the Werich syndicate.

They'd come to see a travel agent whose twin specialties were pain and misery.

The company was called Východni Sliby, which Reynek translated as "Eastern Promises." Bolan got the reference to a film released some five or six years back, dealing with Russian mobsters and their role in human trafficking. Presumably it was supposed to be an inside joke, but Bolan wasn't laughing.

The man in charge of Eastern Promises was Itzhak Feuerstein, whose spotless record seemed to agitate Reynek more than Feuerstein's involvement in the flesh trade.

"Never once arrested," Reynek said, shaking his head. "Not once, and he is forty-one years old! You understand that he's never even paid a fine, much less spent time in prison. Never even held for *questioning.* You tell me how it's possible!"

Bolan kept quiet. He knew Reynek's anger was directed at his fellow officers, the prosecutors who were paid to do a job but wound up sitting on their hands instead, and every other member of the system that allowed cruel exploitation of the innocent for profit.

"Never once," Reynek repeated through clenched teeth.

"Until today," Bolan reminded him.

"I want to ask him how he sleeps at night," the sergeant said.

"Let's tend to business first," Bolan advised.

"*Ano, ano.* Of course."

Feuerstein's place was situated near the airport but distinct and separate from it. Bolan parked beside a Hyundai ix20 mini-van and let Reynek climb out before he locked the Volvo with the button on his key fob.

"Looks like he's got customers," Bolan observed.

"I'll deal with them," Reynek replied, palming the wallet that contained his badge and PCR ID. Bolan stood back and let him lead the way.

Inside, the office looked like any other travel agency. Walls papered with seductive scenes of beaches shot at sundown, jungles caught at dawn, ski slopes and nubile divers wearing next to nothing as they plumbed tropical seas. The decorator hadn't gone with pics of naked children, women bound and gagged, or any of the other offerings concealed behind the perfectly mundane facade of Eastern Promises.

A couple in their late twenties or early thirties sat together, holding hands before a desk whose occupant appeared to be in charge. The nameplate cinched it: Itzhak Feuerstein. Reynek moved toward the customers, showed them his badge and spoke tersely to them in Czech. They paled, then rose as one and fled the office, hands still interlocked.

Feuerstein popped to his feet, red-cheeked, to challenge Reynek in their native language. Reynek answered, "English, if you please, for my friend's benefit."

Feuerstein switched tongues without missing a beat. "What is the meaning of this outrage?" he demanded. "Why have you—"

"*You* are the outrage," Reynek cut him off. "It's outrageous that you live and operate in Prague. In fact, I'm outraged that you live at all."

"Are you insane?" Feuerstein demanded. "Let me see that badge and warrant card again!"

Instead, Reynek showed Feuerstein his back, studied the door for several seconds, then secured its lock. He checked a sign that dangled from a rubber suction cup, advanced the small hand on a faux clock with his index finger, then replaced it with what Bolan took to be the closed sign facing outward.

Feuerstein's cheeks had gone from red to something like maroon. Bolan hoped that he wouldn't topple over from a stroke before they had a chance to talk.

"You work for Lida Werich," Reynek told the travel agent when he turned back from the door. "You're going to explain the details of this operation, with the names and contact information of your customers, then we'll proceed to other facets of the syndicate."

"You *are* insane!" Feuerstein said. "I don't know any Lida—"

Reynek drew his pistol, and the older man forgot whatever he had planned say. Instead, he whined, "You can't do this."

"And who will stop us?" Reynek asked him with a chilling smile.

"You recognize my voice?" the caller asked.

"Of course," Werich said.

"I'm in Přední Kopanina at the moment," he continued. "At Východni Sliby."

Werich felt a slight, unpleasant tingling at her nape, as if a spider's leg had brushed against the soft hairs there. "What brings you there?" she asked.

"Someone has killed the Jew," her caller said, still shy of speaking any names. "From what I've seen, they also searched his files and his computer's hard drive."

"*Sakra!* Are you sure about the hard drive?"

"Let's just say that when I got here, the computer was midway through presentation of a slide show that looked very... interesting."

Werich felt her stomach tighten. "I assume you turned it off?"

"For all the good it did," her caller said. "The two responding officers saw it, of course, together with my partner and our captain."

"*Mrdat!* I'll need their names," she said.

"Not on a cell phone," he replied.

"Then find a landline, damn it! And be quick about it!"

Werich's mind was already focused on damage control as she broke the connection. No friendly farewells to the *detektiv* who doubled his paycheck each month by reporting to her from inside Prague's municipal police force. He was a tool, not a friend, entitled to nothing beyond his base salary.

The same was true of Itzhak Feuerstein, although he was—correction, *had been*—a more valuable tool. The sex tours he'd arranged brought paying customers to Prague, while sending native Czechs around the world to sample more exotic pleasures at a safe distance from home. Whoever had eliminated Feuerstein quite obviously meant to harm their business, too. Why else rifle his files and leave his laptop streaming its forbidden images for all to see?

"Murton."

She spoke the name as if it were a curse that left a foul taste in her mouth.

Werich had few regrets in life, but one was letting Murton live after he fell into her clutches. She'd believed he was secure and could be safely questioned at her leisure, made to suffer at the same time for his rank impertinence, but now she recognized her critical mistake. A parent's fury, even when her soldiers had presumably debilitated him, would never wane as long as he survived.

And his accomplice…well, that problem might be even worse.

It was one thing for a father to come searching for his child—almost predictable, in fact, considering the father's background. But when *someone else* appeared to rescue him, it substantiated fears of a conspiracy.

And Werich still had no idea who else was involved.

She knew that Murton was the chief of corporate security at a big oil company. He would have employees skilled in covert tactics, self-defense and so on, but how many of them would fly halfway round the world to save his life and kill on his behalf? That kind of dedication hinted at a personal connection or, in the alternative, suggested that some agency still unidentified had taken an official interest in the matter.

Fluent in profanity before she'd learned to read and write, Werich unleased her full vocabulary, filling the chilled air of her private office with obscenities that would have made an aged sailor blush. She felt like smashing something, but the office furnishings had cost too much for a raging tantrum.

She would hold on to that energy and vent it later, when the damned American and his elusive savior fell into her grasp. The pair of them would suffer then, along with anybody else she could identify as architects of her discomfiture.

But in the meantime, she had other work to do. If Werich's enemies intended to expose her private business, she must double and redouble her security precautions. Warnings must be issued, bribes enhanced, allies protected, enemies identified and crushed.

The female of the species was more deadly than the male.

If Werich's adversaries overlooked that fact, their negligence would cost them everything they had.

MURTON HALF EXPECTED another reception committee in Prague, but he made it through Ruzyně International without a hitch and charged a car rental from Sixth in the terminal, driving away with a black Peugeot 307. Once he'd cleared the airport and was winding through the streets of Prague, he breathed a little easier.

No badges at the airport told him either one of two things. First, and most unlikely, was the possibility that Pierce remained unconscious and unnoticed in his toilet stall at Charles de Gaulle. The other possibility: Pierce had been found, and the authorities had launched a search for Murton, but they hadn't placed him on the flight he'd booked to Prague.

So far.

Despite his relatively low opinion of the standard-issue "special agent," Murton knew they weren't a flock of total idiots.

Someone would think of Prague eventually—if they hadn't yet—and phone calls would be made. He thought the embassy would be alerted first, and someone there would make the final decision as to involve Czech police or not. As an alternative, if he was still in town, they might call on their pro to look for Murton and attempt to bring him in a second time.

Who *was* that guy?

Matt Cooper, he called himself, but names meant less than nothing in black ops. He was a first-rate fighting man, for goddamn sure. Either an active-duty soldier or some kind of mercenary. Murton wasn't eager to match skills against him, but it shouldn't be a problem. First time out, he'd been a prisoner and someone obviously told his unexpected savior where to find him. This time, free and acting on his own, dodging the pitfalls that had snared him on his maiden voyage into Prague's dark underworld, Murton would be a fleeting shadow. Let the big American try to pin him down.

Before he started any kind of razzle-dazzle, though, Murton had to replace the weapons that he'd lost when he was nabbed first time around. Black-market armorers would not accept a credit card, and Murton was distinctly short of cash. Tapping an ATM would only net five hundred bucks, the daily limit on his card despite the fees he paid to make it "platinum."

Which left him with a single option.

Murton knew better than to visit the arms dealer who'd supplied him for the first round of his Prague campaign. It would invite a squeal to the police or—as he thought more likely—an alert to Werich's goons. Two other names remained on Murton's short list of suppliers, furnished by a merc of his acquaintance who'd done work in Eastern Europe recently. One operation was a hardware store in Old Town, while the other was a pawnshop in the low-rent neighborhood of Vršovice.

Old Town was closer, and he had no time to waste. Each passing moment grated on his nerves like steel wool on a sunburn, while he pictured Mandy in the hands of monsters.

"Daddy's coming, baby," Murton told his grim reflection in the Peugeot's rearview mirror. "Just hang on, no matter what."

He cruised the street in Old Town where his target stood between a barbershop and what appeared to be some kind of campaign headquarters, its windows filled with posters of a grinning man with both arms raised, a pose that brought to mind old news footage of Richard Nixon. Murton boxed the block, checking parked cars along the way for enemies, then gave it up and found his own space at the curb close by his destination.

Walking toward the shop, he braced himself for anything that might occur. What he could not afford to purchase, he would have to take by force. Resistance was predictable, and Murton's injured ribs would be a handicap, but once a Navy SEAL…

No other customers were in the store as Murton entered. The proprietor came up to greet him, craggy features broken by a smile and speaking Czech.

"Sprechen sie Deutsch?" Murton asked.

"German? Certainly. How may I help you, sir?"

"I'm interested in your special stock."

"I beg your pardon?"

Murton dropped a name, saw recognition in the dealer's eyes and didn't stop to think that he was burning bridges for a friend who'd trusted him. The only person in the world who mattered was Mandy. All the rest were obstacles, expendable.

The dealer smiled and said, "I understand, sir. If you'll come with me…"

FEUERSTEIN HAD SPILLED his guts before he died, directing Bolan and Reynek to his private list of customers with "special" needs. The list included mailing addresses, phone numbers, email links—enough, in short, to pinpoint Feuerstein's perverted clients and reach out to touch them where they lived. Somewhere in Prague, the others scattered far and wide with addresses in the United States and Canada, Great Britain, France and Germany, Australia and Japan.

Nearly twelve hundred names in all.

They bought a take-out lunch to go and ate it in the Volvo, parked outside the Myslbek Shopping Gallery, set between Old Town and New Town, on busy Na Příkopě Street. Bolan compelled himself to eat the foot-long sandwich as they talked, despite the queasy feeling Feuerstein's parting words had left with him.

"You think that I'm so bad?" the travel agent had demanded in a fruitless bid to save his life. "You don't think everybody does it, all over the world?"

Well, no. Not even close.

And for the time being, there was one less to make it easy for the bottom-feeders seeking tender prey.

"We can't reach most of those," Bolan observed, while Reynek scanned the list of freaks. "I've got a contact who can tip the FBI to Feuerstein's clients in the States, and they'll contact the Mounties, up in Canada. If we provide the other names to Interpol, they should be able to connect the dots."

"And those in Prague?" Reynek inquired.

Three dozen names, at least. All active pedophiles, according to the travel agent, though he claimed they did their hunting far from home.

As if that made a difference.

"Report them to the PCR," Bolan suggested, "if you think that it will get results."

"I can't be sure," Reynek replied, sounding disgusted.

"Then I'd say we have two options left. One way to go, drop by and visit them ourselves, which stalls our move on Werich's operation."

"Or...?"

"Gamble and feed the media their names. TV, the major newspapers. With any luck, someone will grab the ball and run with it. Find out how germs like living in the spotlight."

Reynek smiled at that. "I like it," he declared. "I know a crime reporter with the *Prager Zeitung* and a news anchor at Prima Televize. They'll take the information seriously and investigate it, if it comes from me."

"Okay," Bolan said. "We can find a copy shop and fax the other lists to Washington and Interpol headquarters in Lyon."

It was a sideshow to the main event, but smoking out twelve hundred child molesters definitely counted as a public service.

Whether any of the scabrous lot wound up in prison wasn't Bolan's call—but he could always keep a copy of the list for future reference. A little something for the road on his travels.

And who could say when one of them might meet the Executioner?

"Then, back to Lida Werich," Reynek said.

"I wouldn't want to keep her waiting," Bolan granted.

Back to Werich and the missing child, if there was any hope at all of finding her alive.

Far stranger things had happened, but he wasn't counting on it. False hopes benefited no one, in the long run. In the short term, though, it didn't hurt to have a goal.

Bolan had two.

Retrieve the young girl if possible. And punish her abductors, either way.

Only one thing was guaranteed: Prague, the tarnished "Golden City," could expect to see more blood.

ONCE HE WAS ARMED, Murton began his search in Perlovka, the unofficial red-light district thriving between Narodni Trida and Stavotske Divadlo, flanked by Old Town on the north and New Town to the south. He didn't count on finding any streetwalkers at large in broad daylight, but blogs available online listed addresses for the best-known brothels operating in the neighborhood. Despite the fact that all were technically illegal, nothing he had seen so far in Prague suggested that the local cops were overzealous in pursuit of pimps, madams or working girls, much less their paying customers.

Murton went slowly, took his time, assuming that by this point his name and face were known to anyone associated with the Werich syndicate, and perhaps beyond that. He had been photographed soon after he was bagged the first time, cell phones snapping photos of his face before the sluggers went to work on him, but whether he'd be recognizable to anyone who'd glimpsed those shots presumably depended on the circumstances of the viewing and how much attention they had paid.

No matter.

Murton wasn't using his own name and didn't plan to ask about his daughter. Not until he'd found someone he thought might have the information he required, that is. But when they were alone and had a chance to talk in private...well, all bets were off. He *would* have answers then, no matter what it took to wring them from the pigeon he selected for interrogation. And if two or three or more were needed to complete the inquisition, then so be it.

Working the streets in any town is more or less the same. You need to find a guy or gal who knows a guy or gal who knows another guy or gal, and so on, up the food chain to the character you're after. Every outlaw operation, big or small, requires some kind of hierarchy. Worker bees exhaust themselves in service to the hive, all for the benefit of one. A king or queen who rules the roost.

Murton had tried the obvious his first time out, asking police for Lida Werich's address, getting blank stares in return. His next step, nearly fatal, had been asking that same question on the streets of Prague. It was a rookie's error, born of panic for his missing child, but he had managed to survive with some assistance from an unexpected source. Back on his own again, a bruised but wiser man, Murton would not repeat the same mistake.

Step one: he hired the ugliest, seediest taxi driver he could find and posed the questions that seemed normal for a horny tourist on the town, with time to kill and cash to burn. The cabbie smirked and offered names. This pimp had mostly Asian girls, another dealt primarily in Africans, and so on. Mention of a younger clientele produced a snicker and a leer reflected in the taxi's rearview mirror.

"For the little ones," his driver said, "you want Alén Konůpek, at Klub Říši Divů."

Club Wonderland.

Of course, it was closed until evening. But if you wanted to reach Konůpek before then—

Murton did.

The man lived in a flat off Října Street, in Old Town, up two flights of stairs in a three-story building with no elevator. Having ditched the cabbie, Murton wasted no time driving to his destination, well aware that his informant might try double-dipping with a heads-up to Konůpek.

As it was, though, he surprised the pimp—woke him, from all appearances, and brought him to the door with grumbled curses on his lips. The pistol Murton showed him ended that phase of the conversation. Murton shoved his way inside and locked the door behind him, verified that Konůpek spoke German and proceeded to confirm that no one else was lurking in the small apartment's other rooms. That done, he steered Konůpek toward a swaybacked couch.

"Sich setzen," he commanded. And when Konůpek was seated, said, "We need to have a little chat."

8

The sat-phone link was clear, six hours earlier in the Virginia suburb of Washington, D.C., where Hal Brognola answered on the second ring, clearing his throat before he spoke.

"Don't ask me if I have Prince Albert in a can," he growled.

"I hadn't planned to," Bolan answered.

Sounding wide-awake suddenly, Brognola said, "Hey, what's happening at…nine o'clock? Where you are?"

"We're keeping busy."

"We. Still got your sidekick with you," Brognola observed. A rustling on the far end of the line told Bolan the big Fed had left his bed to seek more privacy.

"It's working out so far," Bolan replied.

"Don't be so sure," Brognola said.

That put a frown on Bolan's always-somber face. "What's up?" he asked, dreading the answer.

"Word from Paris is that your package didn't make the flight to JFK," Brognola said.

"Damn it!"

"I know. They sent some kind of amateur to handle the transition, and he had an accident."

"How bad?" Bolan inquired.

"He'll live," Brognola said. "Whether he'll keep his job or not's another question."

"So they've lost the package altogether?" Even with the phone's scrambler engaged, Bolan preferred to take no chances.

"In the wind," Brognola told him. "If I was a betting man, I'd say it's likely headed back your way. Return to sender."

Just what Bolan needed at the moment. "If it goes unclaimed," he said, "there's not much I can do about it now."

"Agreed. It sounds like one for the dead-letter office."

"We're still working on the smaller item," Bolan said. "No luck so far."

"Maybe it's time to close the shipping operation down."

"I'm leaning that way, too," Bolan agreed.

"Here's something that may help you," Brognola suggested. "You remember when we talked about those junkets?"

Sex tours. "Right," Bolan said. "I was talking to a travel agent just this morning."

"Name of Feuerstein, by any chance?" Brognola asked.

"The very same."

"I don't suppose he mentioned what he's got on for today?" Brognola asked.

"We went another way," Bolan replied. "It must've slipped his mind."

"Okay. I'm not sure whether this will help or not, but there's a charter flying into Prague today, at half past noon your time. I meant to call you in an hour or so, but since you're on—"

"A charter," Bolan said.

"A dozen happy campers on a Gulfstream IV from Boston via London, booked at fifty grand a head for first-class treatment all the way. The company's Sunshine Charters," Brognola went on. "I'm guessing as in 'Little Miss.'"

"You wouldn't find a Lida Werich on the paperwork, by any chance?" Bolan asked.

"Bingo. That tie in with your deal?"

"It does," Bolan confirmed.

"Hey, is that synchronicity, or what?" Brognola said.

"If you were holding any Sunshine stock, I'd sell it soon," Bolan replied.

"Wouldn't you know, my broker missed it. Maybe next time."

"Has anybody called the local embassy about that missing package?" Bolan asked.

"I wouldn't be surprised if Paris dropped a dime."

"And the post office?" Meaning cops in Prague.

"I doubt it," Brognola replied. "That would invite embarrassment."

"Okay. I'll be in touch."

"Stay frosty, eh?"

"The only way to be," Bolan replied.

A moment later, he had broken the disturbing news of Murton's disappearance to Reynek. "He'll be coming back to find his child," the sergeant said.

"I would," Bolan agreed.

"Are we supposed to stop him?"

"Only if we see him," Bolan said. "Meanwhile, I found us something else."

He told Reynek about the charter flight, its passengers and their arrival time. Reynek considered the information and said, "Nearly a quarter of a million dollars. Losing it would sting, I think."

"Add close to forty million for the plane, if we could take it out," Bolan replied. "I'm guessing that would send Werich into shock."

"A bit ambitious, don't you think?" the sergeant asked. "Considering airport security?"

Bolan had done it once before, a lifetime earlier and far away, before the numbers 9/11 had become a code for tragedy.

"You never know," he told Reynek, "until you try."

ALÉN KONŮPEK DENIED knowledge of Werich's address to the bitter end, insisting that he only had a cell-phone number, which he finally provided after thirty minutes of interrogation. Werich always told him when and where to meet her, Konůpek insisted. He was not among the privileged few who knew where the black widow lived or kept her headquarters.

But there was something else.

Around the sixty-minute mark, when Murton had been tiring from his labors and was worried that the neighbors would begin to wonder what was happening in Konůpek's apartment, the pimp offered a gem in a last-ditch attempt to secure his release.

Sunshine Charters. A service provided for A-list customers who could afford it, including pampered travel and assurance that their every sick desire would be fulfilled upon arrival. Bookings averaged fifty grand, American, and some cost more, depending on the patron's special kink. With no holds barred on what became of a specific lust object, the price might double—even triple—that. Subtract the start-up costs and jet fuel, factor in the overhead from hotels owned or leased by Werich's syndicate worldwide, and every freak who flew Sunshine Charters was putting thirty-five to sixty grand in Werich's pocket.

That was valuable knowledge. But the real news: Konůpek knew where and when the next flight was supposed to land. High noon, at Prague Ruzyně International.

When the information fell into his hands, Murton had fifty-seven minutes left before the flight touched down.

He thanked Alén Konůpek in the only way that seemed appropriate, by canceling out his pain. A kitchen knife sufficed, and Murton left without considering the downstairs neighbors, who would soon report an ugly ceiling stain.

As for the Sunshine Charters flight, he'd have to give some thought to that. Two approaches came to mind. He could attack the plane directly, or hang back and trail the passengers in hope that Werich might appear to welcome them. That seemed unlikely, when he thought about it, but she might still send a flunky who'd report back to her when the meet and greet was finished.

Might. As in a nagging maybe.

Problems rose to mind at once. A fourth appearance at the airport—and his third this day—gravely reduced the odds of Murton passing through unseen. As far as packing heat into the terminal, it could be tantamount to suicide. Beyond that, Murton faced a possibility that once the Sunshine fliers left the terminal they'd scatter, heading off to different hotels. Track-

ing one group or individual, in that case, made it even more
unlikely that the trail would lead him back to Werich.

No choice, then. It had to be the plane.

More problems.

He took for granted that the jet would have some kind of
logo to identify it, but he couldn't guess which of the airport's
two active runways it would use on landing. Murton guessed
the longer of the two would be more likely, positioned as it was
to take advantage of prevailing western winds. In any case, the
two runways weren't all that far apart; they crossed at one point,
granting him a fair yardstick for reference.

He had the weapon that he needed in the Peugeot's trunk:
an RPG-7D he'd taken from the Old Town armorer along with
other toys. It was the paratrooper's model of the classic RPG-
7, capable of being broken down at a moment's notice into
two component parts. Despite that, it would hurl rocket-pro-
pelled projectiles weighing four to nine pounds at three hundred
seventy-four feet per second. Its accuracy rate, as tested by the
U.S. military, was a hundred percent at fifty yards, ninety-six
percent at a hundred yards, fifty-one percent at two hundred
yards—and beyond that, wishful thinking.

Not a problem.

If he had a chance to make the shot at all, Murton would
be within the launcher's comfort zone. And if he didn't…well,
he'd have to think of something else.

Because, whether he lived or died, he wasn't going home
alone.

REYNEK THOUGHT he had adapted well to Cooper's brand of war-
fare, but he presently had a problem and raised it on the drive
to Prague Ruzyně International. "You understand this is an
act of terrorism?" he asked the man behind the Volvo's wheel.

"How so?"

"Well…think of it. Your plan is to attack—indeed, destroy—
an airliner on the main runway of a major European airport.
What else would you call it?" Reynek responded.

"I've always operated on the standard definition of terrorism," he said. "That's use of threats or violence in pursuit of political aims. You can substitute *racial* or *religious* for *political,* assuming there's any real difference, but it all comes out the same. A terrorist acts to change public policy. That isn't me. Isn't *us*."

"You make a fine distinction," Reynek answered. "I can promise you that the authorities will not take notice of it."

"You're one of the authorities," the big American replied. "What do you think?"

"I think that after this, if we go through with it, we shall be hunted by the PCR, the Prague municipal police and probably the whole armed forces, too."

"Maybe. Or they might get a call explaining what it's all about, around the same time that the media's alerted."

"The media is unpredictable, I grant you," Reynek said. "We might be heroes by the time they're finished with us. But the state will not forgive, Cooper."

"Forgiveness doesn't enter into what I do."

"Say *mercy,* then."

"Same answer. Jan, we're hunting people who have never shown a victim any mercy in their lives. I play by rules they wrote."

"I understand the traffickers," Reynek replied. "I'm with you, there. But this lot, on the plane—"

"They're flying into Prague with one idea in mind," the man said. "To violate at least one child apiece. The stats I've read, the so-called 'straight' molester abuses an average twenty girls before he's arrested. The count for predators who specialize in boys runs closer to a hundred. In the States, they estimate that barely ten percent of child molestation cases result in conviction, and some of *those* get off with probation and counseling. Make no mistake about it—Sunshine Charters is delivering a dozen monsters into Prague at noon today. Who stops them, if we don't?"

Reynek considered that. Twelve predators times twenty victims—or a hundred. Sickened by the images that came to mind, he nodded. Told Cooper, "Yes, you're right. One homicide or fifty, what's the difference? They can only lock me up for life."

"Look on the bright side," his partner suggested. "You might even walk away from it."

But Reynek knew that was impossible. Whatever happened with regard to his arrest or ultimate escape, the knowledge of his actions would be with him to his dying day. As the big American had warned him from the outset of their struggle.

If it doesn't kill you, then you have to live *with it.*

But could he? Was uncertain knowledge of the innocents they might be saving adequate to rinse the bloodstains from his hands and soul? In truth, the soul part did not trouble Reynek much, since he'd been educated under communism and had never been indoctrinated by a church. Whatever waited for him beyond death—if there was anything at all—must be determined by his deeds on earth, if there was any justice to it.

As to that, Reynek supposed that he would have to take his chances when the time came.

And with Matthew Cooper directing him, it might be coming soon

EN ROUTE TO THE AIRPORT, Murton pulled into a shopping mall and stopped at the far limit of its parking lot. He left the Peugeot 307 running, popped its trunk remotely and retrieved two bags that held the launcher and its ammunition. The assembly took less than a minute, and he got back on the road, considering which rocket he should try.

He'd taken six rounds from the shop in Old Town. Two were standard four-pound fragmentation warheads, designated OG-7V, designed to kill or maim humans within a radius of twenty feet. They were unsuitable for use against an airliner unless he had a prayer of taking out the landing gear precisely—which, Murton admitted to himself, he most emphatically did not.

The other rockets in his bag were mix and match. He had one TBG-7V single-stage thermobaric warhead—a "fuel-air bomb," in common parlance—that drew oxygen from the surrounding air to generate a blast wave significantly longer and stronger than those of more condensed explosives. Murton had no doubt that it could stop and gut an airliner, but he continued sorting through his options.

Two of his remaining RPGs were PG-7V single-stage HEAT projectiles, short for *High Explosive Anti-Tank*. Those warheads bore a shaped explosive charge employing the "Munroe effect," which produced a jet of near-molten metal to penetrate armor. His last round was a PG-7VR tandem HEAT round, using two explosive charges to defeat active or multilayered armor, like that found on most modern battle tanks.

Airliners were not armored as a rule, but Murton saw no reason to take chances. He would try one of the PG-7V's to start, and if it failed—or, God forbid, if he should *miss*—he'd still have ample ammunition in reserve. A second shot would limit his escape time, granted, but he had no scruples about using deadly force against the so-called law enforcement officers who had permitted Werich's web of misery and death to spread over the city and beyond.

Aside from Werich's kidnapped victims, Murton saw no innocents in Prague.

Society at large permitted individuals like Werich to supply the twisted needs of animals who preyed on women, children, anyone at all who fell within the murky realm of their sadistic fantasies. Even the legislators who had outlawed such behavior were complicit. Some were as covert predators themselves, more willing to forget about a law once it was passed and the congratulations reaped from voters faded in their memory. How many lawmakers made any effort to discover if their legislation was enforced? One in a hundred? Less?

As for police and prosecutors, in Murton's opinion, if they ever did their jobs, people like Werich would be rotting in a prison cell before they had the time to build a global empire. Vice and crime might never be eliminated, humans being what they were, but large-scale dealers could be hounded out of business, one way or another.

Murton was on his way to teach an object lesson on that

very subject, in the heart of Werich's rotten territory. Acting in full knowledge that it might cost him his life, that Mandy then would slip beyond his reach forever and be lost, he had no other choice. All avenues to Werich had been closed to him by fear or by corruption. After this…who knew?

The evil bitch might come to him, he thought.

So he was building a survival option into his audacious plan. Choosing a vantage point outside the airport's grounds that offered him an option to escape. It could go sour on him, he realized, but he wouldn't know until he tried. And simply scouring the streets of Prague had gotten him nowhere, so far, but one step closer to a shallow unmarked grave.

A part of Murton wished he could've hung on with the men who'd rescued him, but he supposed that their priorities weren't his. For all he knew, they could be out of town by this point, maybe beyond the borders of the Czech Republic, off to cope with other half-baked heroes in distress.

But Murton didn't feel like anybody's hero, hadn't tried to be since he had quit the SEALs to find a private life and build a family. In retrospect, he should have vetoed Mandy's trip to Europe from the start, or failing that, he might have done a better job of tracking her abductors. Too late, for all of that. He couldn't rewrite history to make himself look more intelligent, less rusty than he was.

But since he'd been granted one more chance, Murton decided he could damn well do it right the second time around. And if he couldn't get his daughter back, he'd do the next best thing.

Make her kidnappers suffer as a father suffered, from the loss of his beloved only child.

HIS LONG-DISTANCE WEAPON was the Dragunov SVD—an abbreviation of *Snayperskaya Vintovka Dragunova,* translated as "Dragunov's Sniper Rifle"—but in order to use it, Bolan needed precisely the right vantage point. With its PSO-1 scope, the rifle boasted an effective range of fourteen hundred yards, but for all the knock-down power of its 7.62×54 mmR ammunition, it would require an extra-special shot to stop an airliner.

Forget about the pilots. Bolan didn't have a prayer of hitting one behind their tinted windows, much less both, as they approached their designated runway. Fuel tanks? He'd checked schematics for the Gulfstream IV online and learned that the bird had a tank in each wing, feeding the dual Rolls-Royce engines at a rate of three thousand pounds per hour. A tracer round might set one off, but there'd been none available on Bolan's hardware shopping spree.

The disembarking passengers? He might bag some of them, if Sunshine Charters used a mobile exit ramp, but if they deplaned through the standard Jetway tunnel they'd be hidden. He would have to blindly strafe the tube, as likely to hit airport personnel as passengers.

So, what was left?

On a previous mission he'd used .458 Winchester Magnum rounds to blow a big jet's tires on landing.

What he needed was a decent sniper's nest somewhere outside the fence at Prague Ruzyně International but still within the charmed three-quarters of a mile where he could work dark magic with the Dragunov. It looked like tires or nothing, and he couldn't just blow one for the desired result.

"Look for a hill or ridge outside the fenced airport perimeter," he told Reynek as they were circling. "Failing that, I'll need a building tall enough to do it for me, with a runway view."

"Or that," Reynek said, pointing to the massive hulk of a cut-rate parking facility six stories high, built by some enterprising businessman to cash in on the busy airport's overflow.

"Looks good," Bolan agreed and swung into the feeder lane to grab a ticket at the gate.

Five minutes later they were on the open-air sixth level, Bolan's Volvo one of only half a dozen cars up top. He backed up to the concrete wall facing the airport, checked the range and found that they were half a mile out from the X mark where the active runways met and crossed. Bolan checked his watch—

they had ten minutes left before the Sunshine Charters flight was scheduled to arrive.

Cutting it close, but not *too* close.

"Watch out for any company," he warned Reynek as he unpacked the Dragunov and settled in to wait.

9

"I don't care who you've sent to meet the flight," Werich said. "Get more men to the airport *now!*"

Her flunky spluttered, promised to obey immediately. Werich cut the link before he had a chance to stammer out his third apology.

"Kreténe!" she spat into the perfumed office air. If one more person challenged her, however meekly, she was primed and ready to explode. Who would the lucky winner be?

As if on cue, she heard a cautious rapping on the door.

"Enter!"

Otokar Borovský stepped across the threshold, clearly making an attempt to gauge her mood, and said, "Alén Konůpek."

"What about him?"

"He's been found dead, in his flat."

"Dead how?" Werich demanded.

"Stabbed. They say it looks as if he was interrogated first."

"They say?"

"Police."

"Well, *they* should know."

"Yes, ma'am."

"Is that the whole thing? All your great news for the moment?"

"Yes."

"Get out, then."

When she was alone once more, Werich pondered the new development. Alén Konůpek ranked as middle management within her network. Certain information was withheld from him deliberately, letting him perform his duties without over-reaching, angling for a higher post before Werich decided he was ready.

It amused her to compare her syndicate with a Masonic lodge, where new recruits were given basic signs and pass-words, promised more of the society's intriguing details as they rose in rank. Only the grand master—in this case, Werich—and a tiny trusted circle of confederates knew everything about the operation, capable of quoting chapter and verse on command.

Konůpek, for example, knew the details of his job and could identify his two immediate superiors, along with various sub-ordinates, but that was all. He could not steer investigators—or assassins—to the syndicate's headquarters or to Werich's home. He could not contact her directly via telephone or any other means.

What *had* he spilled, if anything, before the knife cut short his time on earth? Each person had a breaking point, as Werich knew from personal experience. Whether Konůpek had reached his, before he died, remained an unsolved mystery.

A more important question: Who had grilled and killed him? And to what end?

The first name on her tongue was Andrew Murton's. Since he was free again, presumably still looking for his daughter and revenge, he was the foremost candidate. Tack on the unknown stranger who had rescued him, and that made two. Hardly an army, but she still had no idea who was behind them or how many reinforcements they might have on tap.

She had police and her own soldiers searching for the damned American, scouring every rathole in the city. Being multilingual, he had better luck evading them than most idiot tourists would have, but she thought his battered face would stand out in a crowd, betraying him on sight. If Murton had disguised himself somehow, the job of finding him would only be more difficult.

Whatever it required, though, Werich meant to see the job done properly. No man defied her in this way and lived to boast about it later. Her mistake with Murton, she now realized, had been the delegation of his questioning to inept soldiers. If she'd taken time to do the job herself, his secrets would be hers—and he would be long dead. No rescuer from the United States or wherever in Hell he'd come from would have snatched her prize away.

Next time, she thought, moving to pour herself a drink. *Next time.*

FIVE MINUTES LEFT and counting. It would be no great surprise if Sunshine Charters missed its scheduled ETA, as most flights seemed to do these days. Bolan wondered if an alarm had sounded after he and Reynek liquidated Werich's travel agent, maybe diverting the flight to another city where the passengers' specific orders could be filled.

But no, that didn't track. The kind of people who paid fifty grand and up for certain pleasures in a certain place would not take kindly to a bait and switch, regardless of the circumstances. Routing them to Bangkok, Subic Bay or Rio de Janeiro would wreak havoc with their plans and might persuade them to abandon Werich's service altogether. More important, would communicate with others of their ilk—by telephone or email, in their dedicated online chat rooms—spreading cautionary tales that could impact the Werich outfit's income in a major way, downstream.

If Werich was the savvy, ruthless businesswoman Bolan thought she was, there'd be no breaking faith with top-drawer customers. The junket would proceed, in spite of any risks, whether she thought Itzhak Feuerstein might have spilled the beans or not. As for the intel from Brognola, Werich likely didn't know that he existed, much less that he'd tipped the Executioner to the arrival of her party animals.

Increased security was possible, either official or from Werich's men, but they'd be covering the airport, not the overflow garage outside its fence. Whatever the response time of police or Werich's soldiers, Bolan believed that he could do his work and slip away before they cornered him. If not...well, his reaction would depend on which side sprang the trap.

"Is this it?" Reynek asked.

Bolan shifted his gaze skyward and saw the jet approaching, readily identifiable by Gulfstream's upward-folded wingtips. As it neared, he could make out the smiling yellow sun that marked its tail, with *Sunshine Charters* painted on the fuselage in flowing script.

"Bingo," he said.

The aircraft circled once, waiting for other, larger planes to clear the runway it had been assigned. Bolan noticed then that when it landed, it would be aimed more or less head-on toward the position where he waited, still invisible to anyone aboard the charter flight. If Bolan made his shot, they wouldn't see death coming. If he blew it...well, same story, with a different ending.

And what, then, if he missed the shot that he preferred? He would accomplish little by peppering the Gulfstream as it taxied, other than drawing uniforms to his position like iron filings to a magnet. Better, he surmised, to simply let it go in that case and attempt to find the Sunshine tourists later, visit them when they were at their ease.

Means to an end—in this case, cracking Werich's confidence and making her aware that he could trash her plans at any time and place he chose. Not literally true, perhaps, but worth a shot.

Speaking of shots...

"They're coming in," Bolan said as he reached for the Dragunov.

EVERY PASSING MOMENT gnawed on Murton's nerves, reminding him again that long years had elapsed since he was combat ready, primed for lethal action anytime of day or night when orders came down from the top. Those years had softened him. Not physically—he'd always followed a strict regimen of exerecise to keep himself in shape—but mentally, emotionally.

The simple acts of loving, marrying, watching his daughter's birth, had softened him. Transformed him from a rock-hard fighting man who rarely thought beyond anticipation of another do-or-die assignment, opening a whole new vista of priorities, responsibilities. He had a family, not merely to support but to protect and nurture. On the work front, Murton also had a reputation to preserve, the polar opposite of his indoctrination as a Navy SEAL, where every move he made was covert and deniable.

What would be left when he got home? *If* he got home?

The business would survive—might even be enhanced by his bizarre adventure, win or lose. Hell, if he wound up dead, it might draw clients out of sympathy alone. Murton's associates could carry on without him, short- or long-term, whether he was serving time or rotting in the ground.

He wasn't sure about his marriage, though. The love was there, but he'd read articles filled with statistics charting breakups after loss of children to miscarriage, to disease, to tragic accidents, homicide. And Murton didn't know if love would be enough.

His wife already blamed herself for letting Mandy go to Europe with her classmates, all the more for talking Murton into it when he was hesitant. He'd tried to reassure her that no blame attached to her; the fault lay with the kidnappers alone, simply for being who and what they were.

But secretly, unspoken to his wife or to the world at large, he blamed himself.

Where was the big bad Navy SEAL when monsters crawled out of the sewer to abduct his daughter, shattering her world, turning her into God knows what? Raw logic told him there was nothing that he could have done, sitting at home or in his office when it all went down, four thousand miles away from Prague. Dad-logic didn't buy it, telling him that any father worth his salt should have anticipated danger, either scrubbing the trip or going along himself, as chaperone.

Too late for second thoughts, yet they were inescapable. His self-torment was worse than anything that Werich's thugs had done to him or ever could do. Meanwhile...

Murton was about to check his watch, when he glanced skyward, saw the Sunshine Charters jet approaching Prague

Ruzyně International from the northwest. He visualized its passengers without their fancy suits and haircuts, manicures and face-lifts, harking back to *The Picture of Dorian Gray.* If all their crimes were manifested in the flesh, strangers would scream and flee before them on the street. They would be barred from stylish country clubs and condos, forced to live in filth approximating what resided in their souls.

Too much to hope for, Murton realized, but he could still expose them to the scorn of civilized society, even if some were not alive to feel its crushing weight.

Smiling, he raised the Russian rocket launcher to his shoulder, peering through its telescopic sight.

BOLAN WAS ZEROED IN ON the Gulfstream IV as it touched down, preparing for his long shot at the landing gear beneath its nose. His index finger was already taking up the trigger slack when Reynek mouthed an expletive in Czech and something like a minicomet streaked across Bolan's left-hand peripheral vision.

The rocket—what else could it be?—struck just behind the cockpit on the starboard side, where the schematics he had viewed told Bolan it should penetrate the forward lavatory. It exploded in a cloud of whitish smoke, the aural thunderclap delayed by Bolan's distance from the blast. Before it reached his ears, he could see flames inside the Gulfstream, visible through the half-dozen oval windows facing him.

He lifted off the gun sight, lowering the Dragunov, and turned to spot the shooter, backtracking the rocket's path. There, on a kind of ridge—a grassy knoll, in fact—a car sat glinting sunlight from its chrome. Behind it crouched a human figure, shrunken by the distance, until Bolan swung his rifle toward the knoll and framed the shooter with the Dragunov's four-power telescopic sight. Bolan caught just a glimpse of profile as the man shouldered his launcher for a second shot.

Murton.

He had reloaded quickly, counting on his first rocket to slow the Gulfstream's progress to a crawl. Smoke poured out off the ruptured fuselage downrange, but the wounded jet kept creeping toward the terminal. Bolan thought the pilots might be dead, stunned at the very least, but the jet's twin engines still provided thrust enough for forward motion at a walking pace.

Bolan had no idea if it could reach the terminal, at least three hundred yards away, but if it did—and if the fuel tanks blew there—it could be a major-league catastrophe. He pictured passengers crowding along the windows facing toward the runway and the smoking Sunshine Charters jet. Would they be smart enough to flee as it drew nearer? If its tanks blew on the way, would shrapnel and the blast's concussion injure hundreds?

He considered spotting Murton, dropping him before he loosed the second RPG, then let a crucial moment pass to see what happened next. He saw a puff of smoke, the launcher's back flash searing grass atop the ridge, then watched the second rocket speed away to find its target. This one struck approximately where the starboard wing and fuselage were joined, touched off the wing's fuel tank and turned the Gulfstream IV into a blazing funeral pyre, stopped dead as secondary blasts ripped through the cabin and it was consumed.

"My God!" Reynek muttered as if from a distance and repeated it. "My God!"

Bolan saw Murton scrambling to his car, tossing the launcher into its backseat without regard to carpet or upholstery. The man slammed that door, ran around the other side and slid into the driver's seat. Then he was rolling, leaving tire tracks in the grass—and none too soon, as Bolan saw a pair of SUVs racing along a nearby access road to intercept him.

Not police, he thought. No flashing lights, no sirens.

"Time to go," he snapped at Reynek as he stowed the Dragunov and put himself behind the Volvo's steering wheel.

Another chase for Murton's sake, and who could say how the pursuit might end.

MURTON WAS BACK ON ASPHALT, running smoothly, when he saw the two black SUVs behind him, gaining ground. He checked for flashers on their roofs, dashboards, behind the grilles, and saw nothing to mark them as official vehicles. Smart money said they would be Werich's men, with orders to eliminate him if they couldn't bring him back for more interrogation.

Murton had two weapons on the shotgun seat, within arm's reach. The larger of them was a ČZW 438 M9 submachine gun, chambered in 9×19 mm Parabellum. The other, a CZ 85B semiautomatic pistol, was chambered for the same ammunition, holding sixteen rounds in its box magazine compared to the SMG's thirty. With one round ready in each weapons chamber, Murton had forty-nine chances to stop his pursuers before he had to reload.

He hoped that would be good enough—and that the gunmen chasing him had rotten aim.

It stood to reason that there would be watchers waiting at the airport, covering the Sunshine Charters flight. He guessed that Werich couldn't ask the cops for help—at least officially—without disclosing why she thought the plane might be at risk. Whether she'd been expecting him to make a move or not, the clients he'd left roasting on the runway had to be high rollers of a sort. She would feel their loss and seek a special vengeance.

And she might start making critical mistakes.

Which would do Murton no damned good at all if he was killed trying to get away from Prague Ruzyně International. He thought his Peugeot 307 might be able to outrun the SUVs, or outmaneuver them in traffic, but he guessed there were at least two men behind each chase car's tinted windows, maybe even four or five. With those odds, Murton knew he couldn't stop and fight them on the roadside, much less in the heart of Prague. Even if he survived, the cops would have him marked, maybe surrounded, before he could make a second getaway.

Thinking of cops, he craned his neck to check the sky above for helicopters from the airport, but it proved a futile exercise. The Peugeot didn't have a sunroof, and its windows wouldn't grant a broad view of the sky while he was busy running for his life. He had to focus on the moment, do his best to stay alive.

For Mandy's sake.

Behind him, Murton saw a shooter leaning from an open window on the first chase car in line. He gave the punk a chance to aim, then whipped the Peugeot's wheel to veer across two lanes, spoiling the shot. A clean miss, and wind whipped most of the sound away behind him.

Lucky once, but for how long?

He reached out to the shotgun seat and double-checked the safeties on his pistol and the SMG. Both cocked, unlocked, ready to rock and roll.

One last attempt at speed, before he switched to killing mode.

He checked his rearview, saw a fourth car join the racing caravan and hoped whoever was behind the wheel had brains enough to stay out of the firing line.

MACK BOLAN FELL IN LINE behind the second SUV that was pursuing Murton, just in time to see a shooter in the lead car open fire on Murton's smaller vehicle. That, and the absence of official license plates, confirmed Bolan's initial feeling that these weren't police.

So, no holds barred.

"Can you take out the tires on this one?" Bolan asked Reynek.

"I believe so," Reynek answered, shifting to obtain a better angle with his submachine gun as his window powered down.

"Okay," Bolan said. "Here's your shot."

He checked his mirrors, swung out to the left and held his speed steady to keep up with the second chase car. After Reynek made his shot—*if* he could make it—Bolan had no method of predicting what would happen with the target vehicle. It might come to a screeching halt, veer off to left or right erratically, or even flip and roll. If *that* happened, the roll should come toward Bolan, where the flattened tire or tires would be.

All supposition until Reynek did his thing.

A heartbeat later he was doing it, the submachine gun hammering short bursts at the pursuit car. Bolan knew Reynek had scored when the SUV began to fishtail crazily, the driver fighting for control. He lost it, and the black hulk flipped into a left-hand roll, while Bolan swung off to the right and cleared its undercarriage by a yard or less.

He didn't bother watching in the rearview while the chase car rolled twice, then wound up on the highway's shoulder, upside down and facing back in the direction it had come from, toward the airport. Whether those inside survived or not held no interest for Bolan. They were mercenary killers who had played a rugged game and lost.

Which left one SUV, still matching every move of Murton's in his smaller car. If anyone inside the leading SUV had seen their cohorts crash, they gave no indication of it, certainly displayed no inclination to go back and help the injured. They were focused, which told Bolan they were pros, but that they also might possess a blind spot.

Roaring into it, he told Reynek, "Same deal, round two."

"Yes," Reynek said and let it go at that.

But as they swung into the left-hand lane, a shooter's head and arms protruded from the SUV's rear window on that side, angling to meet them with an automatic rifle. Reynek saw the danger, fired a short burst at the dangling sniper, but his rounds were lost as Bolan veered back into line behind the chase car.

"We take them from behind," Bolan said as he drew his ALFA automatic, switched it to his left hand and extended it through his own open window.

"Good," Reynek said, craning for a shot from his side.

They cut loose in unison, emptied both weapons in a storm of rapid fire that drilled the SUV's rear window and its tailgate, knocking shiny divots in the jet-black paint. Bolan had no idea whether their rounds had found the driver, simply panicked him or wreaked some other kind of havoc in the chase car. Whatever the case, it tried to swerve hard right and failed, went over on the driver's side and started sliding down the highway's center stripe, obstructing parts of both lanes as it went.

Bolan was forced to slow and make his way around the wreck with two wheels on the gravel shoulder of the road.

Emerging from its cloud of dust, he heard Reynek's curse and saw its cause.

Murton was gone. He'd given them the slip—again.

10

Captain Karel Turek felt his stomach grumbling, not from hunger, even though the noon hour had passed and he had missed his lunch. This was a nervous stomach, something that embarrassed him from time to time, at stressful moments. He had pills to counteract it, but they were at home in his medicine cabinet, where they could do him no good.

Why should he have expected that he would be summoned to a meeting with the likes of Lida Werich? Then again, why not?

As he approached the designated meeting place—a small boutique in New Town, where he'd told his driver that he must pick up a present for his dear wife's nonexistent birthday—Captain Turek corrected himself. To his knowledge, there was nobody else on earth like Werich. In a field where all the sharks were male, had been forever, one sleek barracuda had carved herself a niche at the top.

Or at the bottom, if you chose to look at it that way.

In any case, when Werich called, Turek responded with alacrity. Refusal would have jeopardized his monthly envelope of cash, and so much more that Turek did not care to think about.

As they approached their destination, every parking slot filled at the curb, Turek ordered his driver, "Double-park in front and wait for me. I'll get the door myself."

"Yes, sir!"

Inside the shop, he gave the false name he'd arranged with Werich to a waif behind the register. She smirked at him, sparking an urge in Turek to slap her face, and said, "Straight back and through the curtain, *Dědeček*."

"If I *were* your grandfather," Turek replied, "you would have learned some discipline."

"I'm sure," she said and yawned.

Fuming, Turek moved through the store and found the curtain, which turned out to be a screen of dangling beaded cords. They rattled like old bones as he pushed through them, to find Werich seated at a small card table, flanked by two weight-lifter types with weapons bulging underneath their jackets.

"This is not your kind of place," Turek observed as he sat in the sole remaining chair.

"It must be," Werich told him, "since I own it."

"You should fire the little snot-nosed bitch out front," he said.

"You mean my sister?" Werich asked. She waited for his face to blanch, then laughed. "Oh, wait. I haven't got a sister."

"Most amusing."

"Yes, from where I sit," she said, before her face and voice turned stone-cold. "But I'm not laughing over what just happened at the airport, *Kapitán*. Are you?"

"You mean, the—"

"Was there more than one catastrophe today?" she interrupted him.

Surprised, he said, "I didn't know you were—"

"My plane. My personnel. My customers. Do you have any concept of the loss I've suffered here?"

"I can't begin to—"

"What?" she cut him off again. "Perform your job? Maintain a basic standard of efficiency? Earn all the money that I've handed to you in the past six years? What is it that you can't begin to do?"

"A search is under way for Andrew Murton," Turek answered stiffly.

"It appears you missed him at the airport, *Kapitán*."

"If he's responsible for the attack," Turek replied.

"You doubt it?"

"Terrorists appear more likely to—"

"Attack a private charter flight? The smallest in sight? Is that what you believe?"

"If I had known the plane was yours—"

"I don't report to you," she told him. "*You* report to *me*."

He nodded. Did not trust his voice to answer.

"And I will expect your next report before the sun sets on this day," Werich said. "Telling me that you've caught Andrew Murton or that at the least you know where to find him. Seriously, *Kapitán,* how difficult can finding one man be?"

"In Prague? I think you underestimate—"

"Do it!" she bellowed at him, stunning Turek into silence. "Now! Get out!"

Face flaming, Turek left the small back room and fled the shop, trailed by the clerk's mocking farewell: "Goodbye, *Dědeček.*" Her laughter trailed him as he lunged into the street.

FOLLOWING MURTON'S ROUTE failed to reveal where he had gone. Each intersection on the six-mile drive from Prague Ruzyně International into the city's center offered alternate escape paths. Even with an electronic tracker on his car it would have been a daunting task. Without one, Bolan knew that spotting him by luck alone was virtually impossible.

"We must see with his eyes," Reynek suggested. "Think with his mind."

"Okay," Bolan said. "What he wants most is his daughter, but he can't find her without insider information. If he had that, why waste time with all the airport fireworks?"

"He's still searching," Reynek granted. "I believe it may be hopeless, but I have no child to lose. A father may feel differently. Bound to try, at least, regardless of his chances."

"And if Murton doesn't get the information, if he can't find Mandy—"

"He will seek revenge against the parties he believes to be responsible." Reynek finished the thought. "At least, I would."

Bolan, who'd done exactly that when he was put in Murton's place, replied, "So he'll be after more intelligence. He can't use the authorities, which means he has to work the streets."

"Last time," Reynek recalled, "he did not fare so well."

"He's not a quitter, though," Bolan allowed. "I'll give him that."

"Perhaps we should define our own objective," Reynek said as they passed through the Old Town Square, flanked by a palace and a looming church.

"What do you mean?" Bolan asked.

"First, are we searching for the man or for the child?"

"I'd like to find them both," Bolan said, hedging. "But I came originally for the father."

"And that mission was accomplished," Reynek said, "until some *šašek* lost him in Paris. Has the plan changed, now? Are you still supposed to rescue him? Or would your government simply prefer that he was stopped?"

Bolan had to consider that. Murton was an embarrassment to some in Washington, likely a hero to the grassroots population for his efforts to retrieve his daughter where police and diplomats had failed. As Brognola had said, in Arlington, it was an action movie come to life. And anyone who'd ever lost a child or lived in fear of losing one likely was rooting for the hero.

"If we find him," Bolan said, "and that's a big *if*, I don't see him coming quietly."

"Nor I," Reynek said. "So, my question is the same—what do we do, in that case? Kill the man or join him?"

"He's an amateur," Bolan said.

"But a gifted one, from what I've seen," Reynek replied.

Who would be dead, or back in Werich's custody, if Bolan and the sergeant hadn't intervened to get the chase cars off his tail.

"I guess we wait and see what happens if we meet him," Bolan said.

"And in the meantime?"

"Keep the heat on. And keep looking for the girl."

VLADIMIR NEFF SAT AT HIS DESK, inside his office at the Ministry of Justice, facing Captain Karel Turek of the PCR. Before the officer would speak, he had required assurance that their conversation would be private—clearly meaning that it should not be recorded by the deputy minister or any of his minions. Neff had readily agreed and caught the terse exchange on tape, along with all that followed.

"I do not understand why you suspect police may be involved," Neff said when Turek finished speaking.

"Not the whole department," Turek said. "One officer, perhaps. Or two."

"Explain."

"Not all are pleased with the accommodations we provide for certain...friends," Turek replied. "A few refuse to share in the rewards. A handful have resigned but still observe the terms of nondisclosure. None protest officially, but their dissatisfaction has been evident."

"And you believe that one or more of these may be involved with Andrew Murton? May be helping him somehow in these attacks?" Neff asked.

A shrug from Turek. "I will say that it is *possible*."

"I must assume that you have suspects, then?"

"Three names stand out, Deputy Minister. The first need not concern us—he was reassigned from Prague to Ostrava last summer. Of the other two, one works at headquarters, the personnel department, where he's under constant scrutiny."

"So, we are left with only one?"

"A sergeant," Turek said, "with the PCR's Agency for Organized Crime."

Neff felt his stomach clinch. "That sounds...unfortunate."

"His fellow officers describe the man—Jan Reynek is his name—as a *fajnovou*."

"A 'Goody Two-shoes'? Very possibly," Neff said. "But what makes you believe that he's involved with Murton?"

"It's a feeling, sir. He's used to working independently, a sort of self-imposed exile. No one remembers seeing him or hearing from him in the past three days. I've called his flat and cell phone personally, but there's no reply."

"And from that, you surmise that he is traveling with Murton?"

"Sir, as you told me earlier today, we know that Murton was detained by…certain people he suspected of involvement in his daughter's disappearance. He escaped—was rescued, we could say—with the assistance of a stranger whose identity remains unknown."

"Your missing sergeant?"

"I'm speculating, sir. Until we locate Reynek and confirm his recent movements, who can say?"

"Indeed. This must be handled delicately, Captain."

"Absolutely, sir."

"No all-points bulletins for missing officers suspected of acting in concert with terrorists, eh?"

"Of course not!"

"When you find this officer, if your suspicions prove correct…what, then?"

"Clearly, he cannot be returned to duty," Turek said.

"A trial would be embarrassing for all concerned," Neff said.

"I understand, Deputy Minister."

"It's not my place," Neff pressed on for the hidden tape recorder, "to advise you on the discipline applied to any member of the PCR. There are procedures you must follow, under law. But it occurs to me that if this Sergeant Reynek is involved in murder, he may not surrender willingly."

"In which case," Turek answered, smiling thinly, "we will use the force required to halt his spree."

"I leave you to it, then, with every confidence," Neff said. "Dismissed."

MURTON WASN'T SURE who'd pulled his fat out of the fire back at the airport, but he guessed it could have been Matt Cooper and the police sergeant, Jan Reynek, who had saved his ass from Werich's men the first time. If they *were* the ones responsible, and if they'd recognized him in the chaos following the Sunshine Charters demolition job, Murton imagined they must be pissed off.

Too bad.

He might be grateful for their help—*was* grateful, absolutely—but it didn't change his plans. He owed them *his* life, but not Mandy's. She came first, no matter what debts he incurred along the way toward finding her.

Murton heard jabber on the Peugeot's radio about the airport incident, but could make nothing of it beyond mention of the airline, Sunshine Charters. Whatever else the newscasters were saying was lost in a babble of Czech. He took for granted that there would be promises of tireless searching for the man or men responsible, maybe predictions of a swift solution to the case.

In short, the usual.

He heard it all the time back in the States. Sometimes the hype was true, but many other cases still remained unsolved days, years or decades later. If the victim was well-known, or the details were singularly hideous, some cases made the leap to legend. Jack the Ripper and the Zodiac. Judge Crater. The Black Dahlia. JonBenét.

Murton did not intend to see his daughter grouped with that morbid company. As long as he drew breath and had the strength to put one foot before the other, he'd keep searching for her. And no matter what he found, he meant to take her home. He owed her that much, as a father, after failing to protect her in the first place.

But he needed information. Something, some*one,* who could point him to his little girl—or, failing that, to Werich's lair. If he could ask the witch himself, Murton was confident that she would tell the truth. And he would kill her then, whether the message broke his heart or set him free.

In his years of action as a Navy SEAL, he'd never pulled the trigger on a woman, but with Werich in his sights, he wouldn't hesitate. Some crimes were unforgivable, some individuals beyond redemption. You could only do the world a service by eliminating them. If possible, he would have traveled back in time to rip her family tree up by the roots and set the whole damned thing on fire.

Impossible. But he could still exact a measure of street justice for his daughter and the countless others Werich and her syndicate had brutalized. It wouldn't change the world, or even Prague, he realized.

But it might help him sleep at night.

JOSEF PAVEL'S HANDFUL OF FRIENDS sometimes called him Na Buldok, "The Mastiff." No one seemed quite sure whether the nickname was a reference to his appearance—outsize, blocky skull set squarely on a pair of broad, muscular shoulders, tapering to narrow hips—or to his style of fighting. When he came to grips with an opponent or a subject marked for discipline, Pavel was vicious and relentless, sometimes needing others in his pack to pull him off before he went too far.

But Pavel's problem on this day did not involve a loss of self-control. He seethed with anger, and a growing measure of embarrassment, at his ongoing failure to locate the damned American and whoever was helping him raise hell in Prague. It should have been a relatively easy job, but here he was, leaning on every source his street soldiers could think of, coming up with empty hands.

Pavel's frustration would increase the pain his targets suffered when he finally located them, but at the moment *he* was still on the receiving end of Werich's anger. She kept phoning him to ask for updates, as if Pavel might forget to mention if they'd caught the people they were seeking. Then she'd cut the link without a word as soon as he informed her that there was no news.

Her rage was palpable, and Pavel knew that it would need an outlet soon. If he could not deliver someone suitable for Werich to dissect, it could be *his* head on the chopping block. The blonde *fena* demanded loyalty from her underlings on pain of death but would discard them in a heartbeat if they happened to displease her.

And dismissal from the Werich syndicate was permanent, with no retirement plan.

Pavel was sweating one of the informants whom his men had brought for questioning and getting nowhere fast. In truth, he'd given up on asking questions twenty minutes earlier and

had been punishing the little worm for the offense of being ig-
norant. But he was tiring, felt a measure of his wrath relieved
and had decided that he would allow the worm to live.

But not until he screamed again, another time or two.

His prisoner was wailing properly when Vlasta Marvan interrupted them. Pavel sat back and wiped his big hands on a
towel streaked with rust-colored stains.

"Co je?" he asked Marvan.

"The PCR just called. They've checked the sergeant's flat.
There was no sign of him."

"Too bad," Pavel replied. He checked the worm, lifting an
eyebrow with his thumb, and said, "Get this one out of here.
Bring in the next."

They still had two men and a youngish *děvka* in the holding
pen. Pavel had ordered that the girl be saved for last, since he
was working up a painful head of steam. It would be her mis-
fortune to absorb the brunt of it.

Wrong place, wrong time.

Pavel had no reason to think that any of the prisoners held
any useful information locked inside their heads. But if he failed
to make the effort, did not show the proper zeal, Werich might
think that he was slacking. And from there, it was a short step
to suspecting Pavel of collusion with her enemies.

In which case, the next screams that echoed through the
warehouse would be his.

THE DRAWBACK IN PURSUING a committed loner was that no one
else in town knew where he was or what he might do next.
Prague wasn't home for Murton, so he had no local friends
whom Bolan and Reynek could interrogate. Same thing for
family, unless you counted Murton's missing daughter—and
the Executioner would have been double grateful for a chance
to speak with her.

They had been rattling cages, striking here and there at random, like a rogue tornado ripping through the streets of Prague,
seeking a source who could direct them to the girl, to Werich,
even to her second in command. Thus far, they'd interrupted

screenings at a so-called "adult" theater, disturbed the seedy patrons of a peep-show operation in New Town, left two more pimps lying in pools of blood and torched a shooting gallery that Lida Werich kept supplied with low-grade Turkish heroin. At each stop they had grilled whoever they could find for news of Mandy Murton or for Werich's whereabouts.

So far, no go.

It seemed to Bolan that the city's vice network was shutting down. Not going out of business—that would never happen, under any circumstances—but, perhaps, preparing to go deeper underground. Ride out the storm. Reynek translated nonstop news reports about the Sunshine Charters hit and the police response, described in breathless tones as the Czech Republic's most sensational manhunt.

Strangely, they weren't releasing Murton's name. That could mean the authorities had no idea who'd fired the RPGs at Prague Ruzyně International or that his name had been withheld intentionally. Since the second option would subvert a full-scale search for Murton with cooperation from the public, Bolan was prepared to put it out of mind until his passenger explained.

"They may not know that it was him," Reynek said, "but they know he's out here somewhere. If they're hiding that, it means they have a reason to conceal their interest in locating him."

"What reason?" Bolan asked.

"If orders have been given," Reynek said. "Not necessarily from an official source."

"Werich?"

"Why not? It would not be the first time that police collaborated with a wealthy felon, eh?"

Not even close, as Bolan knew from longtime personal experience. In his own war against the Mafia, back home, corrupt police had stalked him more than once to please a local godfather. He guessed that if the law found Murton first, there was a fifty-fifty chance the grieving dad would simply disappear, saving the state a costly trial and sparing Prague's dark underside from public scrutiny.

Part of the problem at the moment: whatever havoc he and

Reynek wreaked upon the local traffickers in human misery, there was a good chance that authorities and Werich would blame Murton for the raids.

"I need a line on Werich," Bolan said.

"Of course, and we've been trying, but—"

"I mean *a line,*" Bolan repeated. "Skip the face-to-face for now. Can you get me a phone number?"

Reynek considered it, then shrugged. "Perhaps," he said. "But it would be untraceable."

"As long as it connects," Bolan replied.

"I don't believe you can persuade her to release the child," Reynek said, "even if the girl is still alive."

The smile on Bolan's face was grim.

"We'll never know unless we try," he said.

11

More rapping on the office door. Distracted from her study of a city map spread on her desk, with colored markings where her property or personnel had been attacked, Werich swiveled in her chair and snapped, "What is it?"

Otokar Borovský entered, his pale face distorted by a look so tremulous that it was almost comical.

"Well?" she demanded.

"It's another phone call," he explained.

"Who from?"

Almost cringing, he replied, "A man. He wouldn't give his name."

"And I should take his call because…?"

"He seems to know things," Borovský said.

"*Kurva!* What kind of 'things,' for Christ's sake?"

"About all our troubles," Borovský said. "And the American."

"Line two?" Werich asked as she eyed the lighted button on her telephone.

"Yes, ma'am."

"All right. Get out!"

Borovský vanished in an instant. Werich raised the telephone receiver as the office door snicked shut behind him, pressed the button and said, *"Haló?"*

"Can we do this in English?" a deep male voice she did not recognize asked.

"Why not," she answered, and his accent clicked. "Some of my best friends are Americans."

"You lost a few of them this afternoon," the caller said.

Mindful of taps and traps, she said, "I don't know what you mean, Mr....?"

"What's in a name?" he asked. "I was referring to your clients on the Sunshine Charters flight."

"A tragic incident," Werich said, "but you can't imagine I had anything to do with that."

"Just booking it, taking their money, setting up the contacts upon arrival."

"You are misinformed," she said.

"Ah. So you're not a parasite who peddles kids and women to the highest bidders for a living? Maybe there's another Lida Werich working in the sewer and I got your number by mistake?"

Her cheeks aflame with anger, Werich literally bit her tongue to keep from screaming at the *kretén* who had insulted her. When she was certain of her self-control, she asked, "Are you responsible for the occurrence at the airport?"

"No," he answered. "*You* are. There's enough trash in the city now without importing more."

She smelled the trap again. Even oblique acknowledgment by telephone of how she earned her living could mean fifteen years in prison. Since she did not plan on living in a cage, she took a deep breath, calmed herself and said, "It seems you have confused me with some other person, or perhaps you've lost your mind."

"The ID's straight," her caller said. "As for the crazy part, you'll have to wait and see."

"Another threat?" she challenged him.

"A promise. What you've seen so far is just an appetizer. But you could head off the storm."

Tone neutral, she replied, "I'm listening."

"Give up the hunt for Andrew Murton and release his daughter."

"Murton? Murton...no, I don't believe that I'm acquainted

with these people. As for hunting or detaining them, it's quite ridiculous."

"Okay," the caller said. She thought he sounded melancholy or perhaps simply resigned to some unpleasant duty. "You were warned. You've made your choice."

A twinge of apprehension needled her. "Perhaps," she said, "if you explained in more—"

The humming dial tone silenced her. She cradled the receiver, angry at the tremor in her hand.

REYNEK HAD GOTTEN Werich's number from a source who "knew things" about Prague. Regrettably, the same informant couldn't furnish an address, claiming that Werich was obsessed with personal security and changed flats frequently, rotating through a series of apartment houses that she owned in Prague. Getting her phone number was easy by comparison, a relatively simple hacking job on the local telecom company's computer system, but the billing address listed in that cybermaze turned out to be a mail drop in Old Town.

"There is another person I could ask," Reynek said after Bolan wrapped his call to Werich, "but it would require a contact with the PCR."

"Another officer?" Bolan asked.

Reynek nodded. "Not a friend, but cordial to a point. He's a lieutenant with the PCR's Agency for Corruption and Financial Criminality."

"Investigating or participating?" Bolan asked.

"A bit of both, I think," Reynek replied. "At the police academy, he spoke of plans to sweep the country clean and wipe out crime. Of course, we'd both had many beers to drink. Over the years, I think he lost his broom."

"It happens," Bolan said. Not mentioning the obvious—that bad cops had to *let* it happen. Had to wade into the sewer with their eyes wide open every filthy step along the way. He asked Reynek, "You trust him even so?"

"I'm not a total *troubo*," Reynek answered. "I've been documenting the indiscretions of my colleagues and superiors for years, against the day when they may try to force me out of the department."

"Blackmail."

"We say *vyděračství*. It is all the same."

"What's the point in staying when your hands are tied?" Bolan asked.

Reynek thought about that for a moment, then said, "I believe you are a man who understands the power of an oath. I made a vow when I received my badge to uphold every law and give my life, if necessary, to see justice done."

"How do you keep a promise," Bolan asked him, "when the people who demand it of you sell their souls?"

"It's difficult, I grant you," Reynek said. "But not impossible. I owe the duty to myself and to the citizens who trust me."

Bolan nodded and said, "I hope you don't confuse your pledge with a suicide pact."

"Impossible," Reynek said. "If I die, how can I enjoy the last laugh?"

Spirit. Bolan was forced to smile at that. "Make sure it's you who's laughing last and not the other guy," he said.

"You had no luck with Werich, I suppose?" Reynek asked.

"Pretty much what I expected," Bolan said. "She's not about to give me a confession on the phone, much less agree to meet and bring along a kidnapped child to hang herself."

"Sadly, there is no hanging in the Czech Republic," Reynek said.

"Figure of speech," Bolan replied. "I've never favored using ropes, myself."

"If—*when*—I have her address, you still wish to visit Werich? With her army in attendance?"

Bolan nodded. "That's the plan."

"MOVE THE GIRL? Where should I take her?" Josef Pavel asked.

"For now, the lock box," Werich said.

Pavel suppressed his first instinct to grimace. He was not a squeamish man, far from it, and had grown accustomed quickly to the worst aspects of human trafficking for profit. Still, the lock box represented a distinct new level of depravity that he found difficult to understand.

Not that he cared, as long as it returned a profit.

"We're disposing of her, then?" he asked.

"Not yet," Werich replied. "Call it her next-to-last stop on the way. She may be useful yet, but if not...*pfft!*"

She made the airy little noise and snapped her fingers as a form of punctuation for it. Just like that, a death sentence pronounced. Pavel said nothing. Werich was not asking his opinion, much less seeking his approval.

"Is there any word on the American?" she asked as he was turning toward the office door.

"Nothing of any use," he said. "Some claim they've seen him, hoping to collect the cash you offered. So far, it's all *hovno*. I've made object lessons of the two worst liars."

"We still need him," Werich said. "This isn't finished until he stops making waves and asking questions."

Not until he's dead, you mean, Pavel thought. He asked her, "Do you still want to question him?"

"Ideally, yes, but don't take any chances with him. I would rather have him dead and leave questions unanswered than let him escape a second time."

"I won't make that mistake," Pavel said.

"If you do..." she said and left it hanging. Clenched her right hand tight enough to make the knuckles crack like small-caliber pistol shots.

"Don't worry," Pavel said.

"I don't," Werich replied. "You worry for me, eh?"

Closing the door behind him, Pavel passed by Werich's bodyguards and struck off toward the elevator. Thinking through his strategy. Moving the girl would be a routine operation under normal circumstances, but the past twelve hours or so in Prague could not be classified as normal. Werich's syndicate—his family, for all intents and purposes—was under harrowing attack. The smallest errand could become a skirmish, blossom into full-scale battle, and—

Pavel cut off that self-defeating line of thought and concentrated on the task at hand. He'd take three men with him, retrieve the child and drive her to the lock box for safekeeping. Werich had said nothing about making her available to the facility's peculiar clientele, so Pavel would instruct that she remain untouched for the time being.

Later…well, whatever happened to her later was not his concern.

Perhaps she could be useful in an unexpected way, as bait to draw her father in and finish him. Beyond that, it was up to Werich what became of Mandy Murton in the end. A swift death or a life of grueling servitude. It made no difference to Pavel either way.

Palming his cell phone, he began selecting soldiers for the job at hand, choosing only the elite. Because his life might well depend on their ability, he would not trust the second best.

FINDING ONE MAN among three million is a task that no police officer would envy. Doubling the number of targets does nothing to help the manhunters, particularly when the search for one fugitive involves a member of the hunter's own department and must be conducted in absolute secrecy. So it was that Captain Karel Turek cursed the teeming city streets as his official vehicle traversed them, damning every useless member of the public whose existence made his task more difficult.

He had not dared to mobilize the PCR en masse to search for Sergeant Jan Reynek. It seemed too likely that some other officers—perhaps only a handful, but enough—would sympathize with Reynek's motives and his actions, if in fact the sergeant had gone rogue. Turek still had no proof of that and told himself they still might locate Reynek drunk and dozing in a whore's bed, but Turek had reached the point where he must be observed by his superiors pursuing *someone.*

Murton had eluded him so far, along with Werich's minions, largely since he had no ties to the community. Most fugitives were captured when they came to visit relatives or could not keep away from youthful haunts. Since Murton had no roots in Prague, and literally no one he could trust, he was a unique animal. Free-floating, settling nowhere that police could find and striking from the shadows like a wraith.

Reynek was different, a lifelong native, but the officers who'd let themselves into his flat on Turek's orders said it looked as if he had not been at home for days. Where did he sleep, then, *if* he slept? If Reynek had a favorite restaurant or any other place to pass the time, it was unknown to those who worked with him. He stood apart from them by mutual agreement and performed his duties without socializing, telling tales or spending long nights balanced on a bar stool.

To locate the sergeant, Turek had called on the PCR's Rapid Response Unit, trained and armed to cope with hostage situations, acts of terrorism—anything, in short, that posed a grave and sudden danger to the public peace. Or, in this case, to Captain Turek's own longevity at PCR headquarters. While the RRU's members were not detectives, they knew Prague as well as any other officers and kept up contacts on the seamy side of life in order to be ready when a crisis came along.

More important yet, they were prepared to pull a trigger on command, no questions asked, and would accept whatever story Turek fed them if they were required to drop a fellow officer gone rogue. That was the kind of dedication Turek needed, when it appeared one of his own had turned against him and the other members of the PCR.

And if it proved that he had been mistaken, after all was said and done…well, Sergeant Reynek could be treated to a hero's funeral, honored for laying down his life to keep the city and its people safe from harm. No one need ever know that the citation was a fraud, like so much else they took for "news" each day.

The more things change, the more they stay the same.

REYNEK WATCHED Lieutenant Henri Meisel cross Frantisku Street against the flow of traffic, heedless of the vehicles that bleated horns in protest, drivers shouting and thumbing their noses as signs of contempt. Meisel remained oblivious and reached the south side of the street without appearing to have noticed any traffic.

Reynek tracked his progress while remaining on alert for any shadows trailing the lieutenant from the PCR's Agency for Corruption and Financial Criminality. He found none and returned his gaze to Meisel, dressed for the occasion in civilian clothes, the bulge of a pistol visible beneath his jacket if one knew what to look for.

If he was in fact alone—if Reynek had not missed a hidden sniper on some nearby rooftop or a snatch team in a van parked on a side street—they would have a chance to talk. Reynek could make his proposition, twist the knife of *vyděračství* as required and then go back to Cooper with Werich's address. Which was not to say that Meisel might not warn her in advance of any raid they organized.

It wouldn't be the first time he had tipped a subject to impending danger. That was part of Reynek's blackmail log, although he wondered at present if anything he'd documented would be truly useful against officers protected by corrupt superiors. His real threat lay in baring what he knew to Prague's news media, rather than trusting the police department to investigate itself.

Reynek stepped from the small boutique where he'd been idling at the window facing Frantisku, revealed himself and raised a hand to make it easier for Meisel. The lieutenant forced a smile and came to meet him without glancing backward as one might do to confirm a tail in place.

Meisel did not shake hands or greet Reynek by name. "Let's walk," he said, "and you can tell me what it is that's so important."

Reynek gave it half a block, then said, "I need a contact address for a subject of investigation."

"Go through Records like the rest of us," Meisel suggested.

"That's not possible."

"All right, then. Don't be coy. Who is it?"

"Lida Werich," Reynek answered.

"Ah. Your bête noire," Meisel said. "Do you wish to send her flowers? Possibly a box of candy?"

"Something on those lines," Reynek said.

"Is it true, then? What they're saying?" Meisel asked him.

"I don't know who *they* are, much less what they're saying."

"That you've lost your mind," Meisel said, "and become a *mstitel*."

"A vigilante?" Reynek echoed, putting on a frown. "I never thought about it."

"Why should I do anything to help you in this madness, Jan?"

"Because you want to help yourself. Preserve your rank and pension while you have the chance."

"You threaten me? With what?" Meisel demanded.

"Details of the Stella Geislerová case, to start with," Reynek answered. "Then there's Kilian Šípek, Bořek Netolický, the Black Cat Club—"

"All right, all right. You've made your point," the lieutenant said. Pausing, glancing up and down the sidewalk, Meisel nodded toward a nearby alley's mouth. "In there," he said. "She has keen ears, and many of them."

Reynek followed Meisel to the alley and inside it. "The address."

Meisel, with his back toward Reynek, spat a number and a street name—then turned back to face the sergeant with his pistol drawn. "I ought to let you go there, stupid bastard that you are," he sneered. "Of course, they've moved the girl. But I have other orders from the top."

"Too bad," Reynek replied and shot him through the pocket of his windbreaker, two rounds from six feet out. Meisel looked startled as he fell into a twitching heap.

Reynek knelt down beside him, bending close. "You're dying," he told Meisel. "Now I ask you, Henri, as your soul depends on it. Where will they take the child?"

A breathless whisper in reply, then silence. Reynek rose and jogged along the alley's length toward daylight and escape.

THE PIMP WANTED TO LIVE, still thought that he might pull it off if he cooperated with the mad American. Murton used that pathetic, fruitless hope to press his questions home and get the answer he'd been searching for in vain since he arrived in Prague. A number and a name, not much. But if the pimp was desperate enough to tell the truth it could make all the difference in the world.

Murton had trailed the captive on his rounds, collecting cash from several brothels, then got tired of it and bagged him as he left a house in the suburb of Libuš. One look at his pistol had convinced the pimp to play along, at first thinking that it was just a stickup. But he became nervous after Murton tossed his money satchel into the backseat and used a duct-tape strip to blindfold him.

Murton found a weedy vacant lot in Zličín, on the farthest western edge of Prague, and parked there. He left the blindfold on his captive as he said in German, "I'll be asking questions. Every lie costs you a finger."

Let him hear the folding knife snap open. Slice a knuckle to remove whatever hope the pimp had that it might be an empty threat.

"You ask, I answer," the pimp said.

"You work for Lida Werich?"

"Ja."

"You know her address?"

"Nein." As the blade came down to kiss his hand, the man said, "She's always moving! The address is only known to two or three top men! *Ich schwöre!*"

"You swear? All right, try this—your outfit has a girl, American, kidnapped last week from a hotel in Prague."

"Ja, ja. I hear of this one, but I have not seen her."

"What have they done with her?" Murton asked, dreading the reply.

"Ich weiss nicht."

Murton began cutting, heedless of the blood and screams. "You don't know? How damned stupid do you think I am?"

"Anhalten, bitte! Very young ones, some they sell and others put to work, you know? I'm not one of the top dogs who is told these things."

"You've heard something," Murton replied. "I know you have."

"There's trouble now because of this one," the pimp said.

"You're in the middle of it," Murton told him.

"*Ja.* I hear a rumor that she's being hidden."

"Where, goddamn it?"

"At a place they call *der kasten verschlossen.*"

Murton translated. "The locked box? What in hell is that?"

"A place you never want to go," the pimp replied.

Murton pressed the blade against his captive's throat and hissed, "I'm guessing you know where that is."

12

"This 'lock box,'" Bolan said. "Would that be what I think it is?"

"If you assume the very worst," Reynek replied, "you would be close."

Bolan had heard the term before, and variations of it. In its present context, it referred to a facility where victims were maintained for "special" high-end customers with kinks beyond the standard range of BDSM sexual activity. Bondage and "discipline," including sadomasochism, came with rules of play for consenting adults: "safe words," first-aid training, "dungeon" monitoring at parties and so on. In a lock box, any brutal fantasy could be indulged—including murder—if the customer had paid enough up front.

"You think they're hiding her or getting rid of her?" Bolan asked.

"That, regrettably, I cannot say. My contact was...unable to elaborate."

"About that," Bolan said. "What are the odds that they can trace it back to you?"

Reynek considered that and said, "I doubt Meisel would share the fact that we were meeting, under the circumstances. If he'd thought he needed help disposing of me, I'd have seen his backup."

"No one that he would have tipped in case it went south on him?" Bolan asked.

The sergeant shrugged at that. "I'll find that out the next

time I report for duty. If there *is* a next time. Meanwhile, we have work to do."

The lock box.

Bolan was far from sanguine about what they'd find there. If the dead lieutenant's tip was accurate—by no means guaranteed, in Bolan's view—they might arrive too late for Mandy Murton after all. It wouldn't be the first attempted rescue that had slipped through Bolan's fingers, and the memory of each one haunted him.

The place they sought was on the west bank of the Vltava River, in Malá Strana—Prague's "Lesser Town" or "Little Quarter." Reynek knew of it by reputation but had never visited the site before.

"I tried to get a warrant once," he said. "It was denied by Judge Grossmann of the Superior Court, due to absence of probable cause. I could not argue with him at the time, since I had nothing but the vaguest rumors."

"Lucky that we don't need a warrant," Bolan said.

"Lucky for us," Reynek replied. "For those inside…I wonder."

"We'll expect security," Bolan said. "Hit it hard and take down anyone who tries to stop us."

"Dangerous for those who can't defend themselves," the sergeant said.

"They're all at risk, regardless," Bolan said. "Just pick your shots and make them count."

"And if we find the Murton child alive, what then?"

"Our best bet, drop her at the U.S. embassy. They'll have a medic on staff who can take care of her or make arrangements for whatever help she needs. Then give the story to the media and hope her dad stands down."

"But if we are too late…"

"Same drill, but lie about it," Bolan said. "Better for him to hate us afterward than hang around and make his wife a widow, when their child's already lost."

"I hate this filthy business," Reynek said. "I'll never get the stench out of my skin."

"You're not responsible," Bolan reminded him. "We're cleaning up somebody else's mess."

"A *mess,* as you say, that I should have started cleaning up the day I joined the PCR."

"Police departments operate on discipline. You did the best you could, within the law."

"Small consolation," Reynek answered, then he said, "Turn left here, at the light. We're almost there."

THE SO-CALLED LOCK BOX looked like any other warehouse on the riverfront, paint peeling from its metal walls and showing rust beneath. A chain-link fence surrounded three sides of the property, surmounted by a shiny coil of short-barbed razor wire. The rolling gate was chained, but Murton couldn't tell if it was padlocked on his first pass. What he *could* see was the guard on duty, uniformed like any rent-a-cop, wearing a pistol and a side-handle baton on either hip.

Climbing the fence was out, and Murton wasn't looking for a gunfight with the guard that would alert whoever might be in the warehouse. Looking for a third choice, he inevitably came back to the river as his simplest point of access. If he could only find a way down to the water...

Chafing bitterly at every wasted second, Murton drove a half mile south and found a public pier that jutted into the Vltava. Aged fishermen with alcoholic faces dangled limp lines into murky water, sipping vodka from the bottle while they waited for a strike. Nearby, he found a roly-poly with boats for rent and nothing in the way of customers. Murton picked out a skiff, paid three times what the boat was worth, deposited his heavy duffel bag into the craft, then settled at the oars.

The half mile back was rough on his broken ribs, rowing against the river's current, but he fought the pain with muttered nonstop curses, pulling in at last beside an old dock where the target warehouse must have taken shipments sometime in its distant past. Murton cared nothing for the history behind it, being focused solely on the rescue of his daughter.

If she was inside.

If she was still alive.

But what if it was all a waste of time? He wouldn't know until he'd found a way inside the place and searched it thoroughly. And if he came up empty, then what? If the pimp had lied to him or simply had been misinformed, then Murton would be no closer to Mandy.

Where would he begin another search?

"She's here," he muttered to himself as he scrambled from the boat after quickly tying it down.

He wasn't dressed for battle—jeans and running shoes, T-shirt under a windbreaker—but what the hell. This wasn't Kandahar or Baghdad, and he wasn't under military discipline. He was a father fighting for his only child.

Tucking his pistol underneath his belt, at the small of his back, Murton quickly stuffed his pockets with spare magazines for both the sidearm and his submachine gun. The remaining items in the bag were P2 stun grenades, the Czech model, which he'd collected from the Old Town dealer on a whim, uncertain whether they would be of any use to him.

I guess we'll see, he thought, leaving the scree along the riverbank and moving swiftly toward the disused loading dock before him.

To his left, against the south side of the warehouse, Murton saw an SUV and a sedan parked, unattended. One of them, he thought, should serve well for his getaway with Mandy.

And God help anyone who tried to stop them.

"It doesn't look like much," Bolan said as he turned into the short driveway before the gate and chain-link fence surrounding the warehouse.

"It's not supposed to," Reynek answered. "On the inside… I suppose we'll see."

A guard in uniform peered at them through the gate's wire mesh, frowning, right hand resting on his holstered pistol.

"Want to do the honors?" Bolan asked.

"My pleasure," Reynek said and stepped out of the Volvo, calling to the guard in Czech as he approached the gate. The sentry gave a curt reply, shaking his head to emphasize the negative.

Before Reynek could speak again, a muffled sound of gunfire reached them, coming from behind—or possibly *inside*—the warehouse. As the guard turned, startled, Reynek drew his own piece from concealment, raised its muzzle to the wire and fired a point-blank round into the head of the distracted watchman.

Bolan had his foot on the accelerator as the sergeant grappled with a loop of chain, released it and began to roll the gate out of his way. He drove past Reynek, steered around the fallen guard and pulled up to the street-side entrance of the warehouse. Reynek dragged the corpse behind a small guard shack, concealed from passing vehicles, and ran to join him at the Volvo, both men taking automatic weapons from the car. Another burst of gunfire from the warehouse added urgency to every move.

The door facing the street was locked, but Bolan took the knob off with a short burst from his Vz. 58 and they were in, confronted by a blank wall with a hallway opening at either end. They split up, Bolan breaking to the left and Reynek to the right.

Bolan reached the corner and stopped before a maze of narrow corridors, the sounds of firing becoming more intense. He picked one hallway, following the sounds, and plunged ahead.

MURTON SUPPOSED the lock box was equipped with an alarm to rouse the guards in residence. It was not audible to him, but he had barely cracked the entry door beside the main bay of the loading dock when two armed men appeared to intercept him. Murton didn't understand a word they shouted at him, and it made no difference. He fired a short burst at the gunman on his right, cutting the legs from under him, then ducked and rolled as number two returned fire with a shotgun.

It was a close shave, buckshot raking furrows in the nearby wall and raining plaster dust. Murton kept moving, nearly prone, while angling for a shot at his opponent. Swallowing an urge to rush the bastard, Murton palmed one of his flash-bang stun grenades, released the safety pin and made a sidearm pitch that bounced the apple-green cylinder off one wall and down-range toward his enemy. Five seconds later, a thunderclap ripped through the warehouse and Murton charged after it, catching the shooter supine on the concrete, hands over his eyes.

Murton pinned him there with three rounds from his SMG, finished the other gunman with another three and moved on, shouting out his daughter's name. Doors lined the smoky corridor on either side, and even with the ringing in his ears, he heard a faint voice answer.

"Daddy? *Daddy!*"

Murton found the door, tried the knob and found it locked. Of course. He knelt beside it, called to Mandy through a slot set in the black steel panel. "Stand back from the door now, baby. To your left. I'm shooting off the lock."

"Okay," the small voice answered.

Murton gave her five, six seconds, then stood back and hit the doorknob with a stream of Parabellum shockers, ripping it away. The door swung open and he leaped inside, half-blinded by a rush of tears as Mandy lurched into his arms.

REYNEK HEARD FIRING INTENSIFY from an adjacent corridor and hesitated in the hallway he had chosen to explore, eyeing the dozen silent doors on either side. He tried two, found them locked and called out in the hope of getting a response, but no one answered him.

Did that mean that the rooms were empty? Or that their occupants were drugged or terrified to answer? Were they dead?

His first impulse was to proceed along the corridor, blasting each lock in turn, searching the chambers built as pens of misery, but Reynek focused on his mission, understanding that his partner might need his help. Reluctantly, he turned away, hoping that when the smoke cleared the police would finally sweep through this godforsaken place, after ignoring it for years.

He doubled back, guided by echoes and the smell of cordite as he turned one corner, then another. Never in his life before had Reynek seen a warehouse that felt claustrophobic. This one had been turned into a warren of small rooms where anything could happen, safe from prying eyes or interruption. Moving through its shadows, he felt heartsick for the horrors it had witnessed and concealed.

But it would end on this day.

Rounding another corner, he collided with a running man and stumbled backward, almost lost his balance but maintained a firm grip on his weapon as he saw a submachine gun swinging toward him. Index finger on the trigger, he had target acquisition when he saw a smaller form beside the gunman, cowering, and heard a voice say, "Christ! It's you!" in English.

Murton let his weapon's muzzle dip, glanced back over his shoulder as the sound of running feet reached Reynek's ears and said, "They're coming."

Moving up to join him, while the trembling girl hid in her father's shadow, Reynek cautioned Murton, "Cooper is here, as well. Be careful."

Murton flashed a smile or grimace, Reynek couldn't say for sure, as he replied, "I've never shot a man by accident."

Dim lighting at the far end of the corridor revealed two men in black running toward Reynek and the Murtons. Both figures were armed with automatic rifles of some kind.

"Not Cooper," Murton said.

"No," Reynek agreed and opened fire on their advancing enemies.

The riflemen both skittered through a jerky little dance, dropping their weapons as they lurched about, careening into walls, then fell together in the middle of the hallway. Reynek did not bother moving in to see if they were dead. It was enough for him that both were down and out of action for the moment, no more threat to him or his companions.

Still thinking of the other bolted doors, Reynek glanced at Mandy Murton, then asked her father, "Could you tell if any more are here?"

Shaking his head, Murton reached down to place a hand on Mandy's shoulder. "I got lucky," he replied. "Call it a fluke or fate, whatever. If you want to check the other rooms, go on. We're getting out of here."

"You have a car outside?" Reynek added doubtfully.

"Not here," Murton said. "Close, if we can make it to the boat I rented."

"Help me find Cooper," Reynek suggested, "and we'll go together."

"Mandy—"

"Will be safer with three guards than one," Reynek said. "But the choice is yours."

He turned away, had covered half a dozen strides before he heard the Murtons following.

"All right," said Murton, coming up beside him. "But for God's sake, make it quick!"

BOLAN DROPPED HIS EMPTY magazine, reloading on the run, just as his latest target ducked around a corner, out of sight. Three dead men lay behind him, with an unknown number of defenders waiting up ahead, while firing continued from another section of the warehouse. Bolan's only consolation at the moment was the fact that Lida Werich's goons weren't likely to seek help from the police.

But they could call for reinforcements. Might have placed the call already.

No time to waste.

He edged along the hallway, clinging to the right-hand wall. Bolan was ready to be done with this, but not enough to die because he rushed unnecessarily. He still had no idea who'd started shooting in the first place, but some of the ongoing fire sounded like Reynek's SMG.

Then again, 9 mm weapons generally sounded more or less alike.

He reached the corner where his enemy had disappeared, crouched down and strained his ears for any sound of movement close at hand, then took a leap of faith. Smooth concrete let him slide, scanning for targets, but the man he'd been pursuing was no longer there. Downrange, a door stood open, muffled cries and squeals emerging from behind it.

Bolan rose and jogged in that direction. He had covered half the distance when the thug who'd dodged him moments earlier emerged, holding a naked adolescent girl before him as a shield, one arm around her neck, the other with a pistol pressed against her temple. Whatever he barked at Bolan in his native language was a waste of breath.

Stalling for time and angling for a shot, the Executioner replied, "Sorry. I don't speak Czech."

The gunman blinked at him. "American? You want the child, yes?"

Bolan took another cautious step forward, thumbing the fire-selector switch on his Vz. 58 assault rifle to semiauto fire.

"The child," he said. "That's right."

"You papa, yes?"

"The next best thing," Bolan replied.

Blinking as he retreated, step by awkward step, the gunman didn't seem to understand—or care, for that matter. "We make a deal, yes? I give you the little girl, and maybe this one, too. You like?"

"I'll need to see the child," Bolan advised.

"Sure, sure. I take you, if you promise me I walk away."

"Why not," Bolan replied, with no guilt for the lie.

"Okay, we deal, yes? Follow me. No tricks, now!"

"Wouldn't dream of it," the Executioner replied.

The shooter backed away from him, keeping his hostage in between them. She seemed dazed, or maybe drugged, her open mouth producing unintelligible mewling sounds. Bolan paid no attention to her nudity, his focus solely on the gunman's weapon and his face, averted every few steps to make sure that he was backing in the right direction.

"Just around this corner, Papa," he told Bolan. "Almost there."

"No tricks, you said," Bolan reminded him.

"No, no! I play you straight."

"Sounds good," Bolan agreed in his most reasonable tone.

He had a fair view off the shooter's head—well, roughly half of it—above the girl's right shoulder and beside her face.

It wouldn't be an easy shot, but Bolan had scored hits at longer ranges, under trickier conditions.

"Now I turn the corner, eh?" the gunman said. "And then—"

"Hold it!" a voice ordered in English.

Bolan thought he recognized it, had no time to think about it further as the shooter half turned with his human shield, clearly prepared to kill her if he found himself with no way out. The Vz. 58 cracked once, its 7.62×39 mm round punching a neat hole over his right ear, exploding from the left side of his skull in crimson mist. The dead man dropped and dragged the squealing girl down with him in a tangle of disordered, thrashing limbs.

Bolan was at her side and lifting her by one arm when he saw Reynek and Murton moving toward him with a girl in tow. Bolan removed his jacket, helped the naked captive into it, her back turned toward the new arrivals. When she'd buttoned it, the hem covered her to midthigh.

"We finished here?" he asked the others.

"There may still be more," Reynek said, glancing back and forth from Murton's daughter to the older girl.

"We'll make a call," Bolan said. "We're already running late."

13

The FBI's legal attaché met Bolan's party at the U.S. embassy on Tržiště Street, in Prague's Little Quarter. A pair of armed Marines stood by but made no effort to search Bolan or Reynek for weapons. Andrew Murton, disarmed on their drive from the lock box, spoke when spoken to and otherwise remained as silent as his trembling child.

"Well, you've got friends," the G-man—Agent Larry Wade—declared. "Before you got here, they were burning up the lines from State, Justice, the Hoover Building. I have orders, and I'll follow them precisely."

"I suppose we'd better hear them," Bolan said.

"First thing, I've got a medic waiting for the little lady," Wade continued. "Dr. Karen Brandt. I've never seen her stumped, but if there's something she can't handle, we're prepared to out-source through the local children's hospital. With strict security, of course. It looks like Dad could use a physical himself."

"I'm fine," Murton replied.

"Okay, then. If you want to take your daughter on inside, they'll see her right away and get things rolling."

Murton hesitated, holding Mandy's hand, turning to face Bolan and Reynek. "Listen, if you're ever in New York and you need anything… Hey, never mind New York. If you need anything at all, ever—"

"You'd better go," Bolan advised him.

"Right. I guess. So long."

Wade tracked the Murtons out of earshot, then said, "I have a fair idea of what's been going on here."

"What more do you need?" Bolan asked.

"At my pay grade? Nothing," Wade replied. "I've felt the urge to go that route myself a time or two. Who hasn't, when it comes to law enforcement. Hell, with 'extraordinary rendition' and 'enhanced interrogation,' we're halfway there already. Maybe more."

"Let's hope not," Bolan said.

"It's funny you'd say that. Why not?" the agent asked.

"Because we need a moral anchor," Bolan answered. "Granted, there are times the rule book doesn't work, but we still *need* the book to keep us honest. Otherwise, it's wild-frontier time and nobody's safe."

Wade nodded. "Sure, I guess. But what cop hasn't dreamed of making one good surgical strike in his time?"

"The thing about surgery," Bolan replied, "is it's only for surgeons. You wouldn't ask a taxi driver or your gardener to do a kidney transplant, would you?"

Wade frowned, then replied, "Most cops have decent training these days, lots of them with military backgrounds. They—"

"That's tactical," Bolan said, interrupting him. "I'm talking mental and emotional. You take your rage and natural frustration off the table."

"Oh? Is that what happened here, with Murton's kid?" Wade asked.

"It was for me," Bolan replied, almost the truth. "I couldn't speak for him."

"Uh-huh. I understand that neither one of you needs any transportation from the embassy, but here's some free advice."

"I'm all ears," Bolan said.

"You're on the radar," Wade told both of them. "I don't know if the PCR has either of your names—hell, *I* don't have your names—but you are absolutely being hunted. Hear me? Not just cops, but traffickers. If I said *open contract*—"

"I'm familiar with the term," Bolan assured him.

It meant that Lida Werich had a bounty on his and Reynek's heads, payable to anyone who brought them in, dead or alive.

"If I were you," Wade said, "I'd catch the next thing smoking out of Prague and out of the CR."

"We've got unfinished business," Bolan said.

"Okay," Wade said. "I tried. Good luck, and give 'em hell."

"YOU DISAPPOINT ME, Josef," Werich said.

Pavel stood ill at ease before her desk and eyed the pistol on its blotter, likely thinking of the other times he'd seen her vent grave disappointment through a gun barrel.

"The lock box," she continued, teeth clenched as she spoke. "Not only lost to us, but in the hands of the police. How many living witnesses, Josef?"

"Only four," he said.

"Oh, *only* four." Her tone like acid on his eardrums.

"Three collected in the warehouse raid," Pavel said. "One left at the Ministry of Justice."

"On the front steps, I believe. *After* the media was summoned."

"Yes."

Her right hand found the pistol. Covered it. "I don't recall the last time that I felt such disappointment," Werich said. "What should I do with you, Josef?"

He mumbled something unintelligible.

"What? Speak up!"

"I said, give me another chance."

"You were impressive once," she said. "I thought so, anyway. But now…"

"I'll find the men responsible!" Pavel declared. "I'll bring their heads and place them on your desk!"

"Where will you look? Why should they still be here in Prague, now that they have the girl they came for in the first place?"

That stumped Pavel for a second, then he said, "Because they hate us. They will want revenge."

"I wonder. If you're right for once, we still might salvage something out of this *zasraný* mess."

"I *am* right. You will see."

"But there is still the problem of my shattered trust in you," she said. "These *darebáci* have outsmarted and defeated you at every turn. How do I know that you won't fail again? Leave everything I've worked for all these years in ruins?"

"I will pledge my life!"

"You've done that. I should claim it now."

He gave a miserable shrug and said, "Who else is there?"

"Who else, indeed? Oh, wait…"

Raising the pistol, Werich fired a point-blank shot into his groin. Pavel collapsed, squealing, his face still visible above the desk. She aimed and fired another round into his open mouth, to silence him.

"I'll do the job myself," she told his twitching corpse.

Her bodyguard, Miloš Týrlová, burst into the office, gun in hand. He visibly relaxed on realizing that the shots had come from Werich's pistol.

"Have this trash removed," she ordered, "then come back to me. You are my captain now, and we have plans to make."

He left, already barking orders as he cleared the threshold, summoning assistance to remove the body. Werich raised the pistol to her nostrils, breathing in the heady scent of gunpowder, and smiled.

She took for granted that the Murton child was beyond her reach by this point. What of it? None of Werich's victims ever saw her face. Nothing the girl or any other lock-box denizen could tell police would damage Werich. The property's deed was held by a shell corporation, a subsidiary of another based in Liechtenstein.

She was untouchable. And yet…

The enemies she faced were not constrained by laws or regulations. They defied convention, thus their movements could not be predicted. She had nothing in the way of leverage to use against them, since they had already liberated Murton's daughter from her custody.

Though it gave Werich a twisted sense of satisfaction that the child would never be the same again, it did nothing to relieve her of her adversaries. Only standing over their dead bodies would provide the ultimate satisfaction that she craved.

Speaking of which, Miloš Týrlová had returned with two strong men to carry Pavel's leaking corpse out of her office.

"Where do you want them to take him?" Týrlová asked.

"Away," Werich told him. "Who cares? We have plans to discuss."

"I HOPE HE WILL STAY on the airplane this time," Reynek said as they drove past the Ledebour Garden.

"I'd bet my life on it," Bolan said, "as soon as his daughter can travel."

"The child," Reynek said. "I don't know."

"Don't know what?"

Reynek shrugged. "Who can say what she's seen, what she's suffered? Or if she will ever be right?" On the last word, he raised a hand, tapping his temple and grimacing.

"Children bounce back," Bolan said. "They survive. If it takes time and money, the family has both."

"Well, it's out of our hands," Reynek said. "Are you done with Prague now?"

"What do you think?"

"I ask because if you are leaving, I must decide what to do," Reynek answered. "Go back to my job and pretend nothing's happened or keep up the fight by myself."

"The first may be an option," Bolan said. "But if you want to stick it out, you're not alone."

"And you are not content, I think, with slapping Werich's hand."

"We've cost her money," Bolan answered, "but I doubt we've really taught her anything."

"She won't learn, that one."

Bolan's cell phone rang and he opened it. He recognized the number on display from having dialed it recently: the U.S. embassy in Prague.

"Hello?"

"The agent had your number," Murton's voice explained.

"Expiring when we end this call," Bolan replied.

"Good plan. Listen, I never really got around to thanking you."

"I heard it loud and clear," Bolan said.

"Well, in that case, count this as a bonus. A going-away gift."

"I'm listening."

"The doctor's in with Mandy now. She wanted privacy, you know? But just before I left she told me something. There's another shipment coming in. You read me? Kids, young women, I'm not sure. At least a truckload, coming into Prague tonight."

"Who told her this?" Bolan asked.

"No one planned to. Seems the cages at that goddamned place aren't soundproof. Mandy overheard a couple of the goons."

"Okay."

"I don't know if you're hanging around," Murton said, sounding awkward, "but just in case…"

"We're on it," Bolan told him. "Have a safe trip home."

He cut the link before Murton could think of any more to say, turning to Reynek.

"What?" the sergeant asked.

"The Murton girl heard Werich's people talking," Bolan said and filled him in.

"Tonight? To Prague? If true, they might be sent from anywhere. They won't be flying, but beyond that—"

"Murton said at least a truckload."

"Fresh meat, possibly," Reynek said. "Shipments come to the CR from other countries through selected border crossings where the syndicate pays customs officers to go blind for an hour or so."

"Same thing as drugs or any other contraband," Bolan observed.

"Except that drugs have not been kidnapped, and they feel no pain."

"Too bad we don't know where they'll be," Bolan said.

"Someone knows," Reynek replied, stating the obvious.

"Right. Thanks for that."

"No, I mean there is a man who keeps his finger on the pulse of such things," Reynek said.

"Where's he been hiding through all this?"

"I only thought of him now. Werich's accountant," Reynek said. "He must keep track of property in transit, eh?"

"Makes sense to me," Bolan said. "Let's drop in and check his books."

CAPTAIN KAREL TUREK took the phone call on his private line and stiffened at the sound of Lida Werich's voice. "I need to know what progress you have made," she said.

Glancing around his empty office as if someone might be lurking there unseen, Turek replied, "I've been coordinating everything with Pavel, as you—"

"Josef is no longer my employee," Werich interrupted him. "You deal with me directly from now on."

Turek was wise enough to stop himself before he asked what had become of Werich's second in command. "Of course," he said through clenched teeth. "If that's what you prefer."

"It is what I require. Now, any progress?"

"As you may imagine, we have been distracted by discovery of a…unique facility in Malá Strana. Busy sorting the corpses and the children who we found there—"

"Never mind that *hovno*, Captain. You know what I'm asking you. What progress?"

"Nothing to report on Andrew Murton or his daughter. Also nothing on the others."

"You say *others?* Plural?"

Turek realized he'd stepped into a trap. "I mean to say the man who helped Murton escape, of course. And now…it may be possible that they have been assisted by a membr of the PCR."

"Indeed." Her tone had gone ice-cold. "His name?"

"I don't think—"

"That's correct," she hissed at him. "You *don't think*. What you do is answer questions when I ask them. Are we clear?"

"I hear you."

"Good. His name?"

"Jan Reynek. Sergeant Reynek."

"And you've lost him now? How is that even possible?"

"It has been some time since he called or showed his face at headquarters," Turek replied. Embarrassment on top of anger and humiliation turned his cheeks a flaming red. His pulse thumped in his ears, a steady drumbeat.

"I require his address," Werich said.

"I've had it checked. There's no one—"

"His address!"

"One moment." Turek had to rummage through the papers on his desk to find it, then recited it into the telephone.

"Fax me his photograph," Werich commanded, reeling off a number while he scrambled for a pen to jot it down.

"All right," he said. "I have it."

"Do it now! And keep the updates coming. Don't make me call you again!"

The line went dead, but he double-checked that no one was on the other end before snarling a stream of profanity into the phone, paranoid that Werich might have tricked him somehow and was listening for any hint of insubordination.

He had a headache. Turek removed a tin of aspirin from his desk and washed four tablets down with vodka. While he let that settle, praying for relief, his thoughts veered back and forth from Werich to his missing sergeant. Turek wished he could get rid of both and thereby make his life much easier. If they would only meet and kill each other, he imagined that the bulk of all his problems would be solved.

If they could meet...

He had Reynek's cell-phone number. One of them, at least. What would prevent him from calling it, leaving a message on the traitor's voice mail that directed him to Werich's hiding place?

Nothing but common sense.

When he considered it, Turek decided that there was no realistic chance of Reynek cracking Werich's syndicate, ever with help from an accomplice. Werich would destroy him—them—and then start looking for the one who had betrayed her. It would be a short list, and she might kill everybody on it, just to hedge her bets.

Too risky.

No, his only course of action was to carry on as ordered, do his best to stop the mayhem that was gutting Prague and get things back to normal. And with that in mind, he had another job to do.

Providing the security for Werich's latest shipment from the East.

AUGUST BERGER NEEDED a vacation. It was too damned hot in Prague these days, and even though he held himself aloof from Werich's business in the public eye, he was afraid he might get burned. Paris was nice this time of year. Or maybe Venice. If he left this evening, he could—

The buzzer sounded on his desk, distracting him. He answered, and the sultry voice of Věra Pojar, his receptionist, came back at Berger from the intercom.

"Two gentlemen to see you, sir."

"Are we expecting anyone?" he asked.

"No, sir. But one of them is from the PCR."

"Ježíš Maria!"

"Sir?"

"Nothing." He took a deep breath, smoothed his rumpled tie. "Please send them in, Věra. And then go on to lunch."

"Yes, sir."

The door opened a moment later to admit a pair of stern-faced men in suits. Věra gave her boss a worried parting look before she closed the door behind them and departed. Berger rose to welcome them, forcing a smile.

"How may I help you, Officers?" he asked.

"We need a bit of information," the taller of the two said.

"And that would be…?"

"When and where are you expecting Werich's next shipment of slaves?"

Berger tried to control the rapid flicking of his eyes between the two grim faces. He sat down, swallowed a lump that had arisen in his throat and said, "I'm sorry, gentlemen, but I have no idea—"

"Your secretary's left," the man said. "We heard you on the intercom."

"And...?"

The speaker's companion drew a pistol with a bulky muzzle, seemed to aim at Berger's face, then fired a shot that stung his ear like fury. Squealing, Berger clapped a soft hand to his wounded ear and drew it back, bloodstained.

"Are you insane?" he asked them, not quite sobbing.

"Possibly," the first man answered. "Nonetheless, my question stands."

"You can't imagine that I—"

Pffut! Another muffled shot was aimed his way, this one burning a track across his left biceps. Berger began sobbing, from fear as much as pain.

"What do you want?" he cried.

"I've told you," the spokesman for the pair said. "Must I repeat myself?"

"No! But the shipment—"

"Think before you lie," the talker said. "We brought two guns and many bullets."

"It's tonight," the terrified accountant blurted out. "Two trucks, arriving from Slovakia."

"What time?"

"Midnight."

"Which crossing?"

"Near Hodonín, from Skalica," Berger said.

"How many passengers?"

"Sixteen per truck. So, thirty-two."

"Security?"

"Well, Lida's men, of course. The normal complement is three or four per vehicle."

"Anything else?"

Berger swallowed again and said, "Police, I think."

The talker scowled at him. "What kind?"

"The PCR," Berger replied.

"And how do you know this?"

"I process their payments," Berger told him. "What could be more obvious?"

"Where are your books? The ones for Werich's operation?"

"In the safe," Berger said, nodding toward a Bedřich Feigl landscape on the wall. "Behind the painting."

"We shall take those with us, if you don't mind," the man said. "Or regardless, if you do."

"Yes, yes. Take anything you like."

Berger got up and crossed the office, took the painting down, opened the wall safe without trying to conceal its combination. Passed two bulky ledgers to the other man without a pistol in his hand.

"It's all in there," he said. Thinking, *My death warrant, as well.*

"Goodbye, then," the talker said.

Berger had a moment of relief, before the silent member of the duo raised his gun and shot him in the face.

14

Hodonín is a thousand-year-old town on the river Morava, in the Czech Republic's South Moravian Region, a hundred and thirty miles southeast of Prague. To reach it from the capital, Bolan started on the D1 Motorway to Brno, where he would pick up the D2 southbound, then watch for I-55 eastbound to Hodonín. Before he reached that destination, though, he would be cutting off on country roads to reach a minor border crossing where Werich's drivers planned to cross at midnight.

Bolan trusted their informant. August Berger hadn't been a brave man, and there was no reason to suspect he'd sent them on a wild-goose chase with his last words. Of course, there was the possibility that Werich's plans might change, in light of recent losses she had suffered, but the Executioner surmised that she'd be anxious to replenish any stock she'd lost during his raids and get her filthy business back on active footing.

Any way you sliced it, if the shipment tried to cross, Bolan would be there. And he'd do his damnedest to derail it.

But with reasonable caution. No damage to the human cargo while he dealt with Werich's shotgun riders. As for any cops assigned to guard the trucks, in violation of the law and their recorded oaths of office…well, that could be a problem. Reynek recognized "Cooper's" refusal to use deadly force against police, regardless of the circumstances, and demonstrably had no such qualms himself. He had agreed to deal with any uniforms that turned up in support of Werich's operation, on the understanding that a large force of police would render their attack unfeasible.

Still edgy at participating in a raid where cops—even the crooked kind—were likely to be shot by anyone, Bolan had stopped in Prague to buy a battery-powered bullhorn. They could use it to announce themselves before the shooting started, maybe warn whatever PCR men might be present to perform their legal duty, and when that failed—as he thought it would—the rest came down to nerve and pinpoint marksmanship.

Their first priority: protect and liberate whatever prisoners were riding in the Werich vehicles. Second: protect themselves. If they could take the cops alive somehow, restrain them and alert other police, maybe the media, Bolan thought they might take a baby step toward cleaning up the PCR.

He also rated that thought as a fantasy.

The kind of "lawmen" who would guard a slave shipment would also kill to save their worthless reputations, keep the gravy flowing from the traffickers in Prague. There'd be no giving up without a fight. And he would have to trust in Reynek's skill to deal with that eventuality.

Or scrub the mission entirely and plan to free the prisoners once they'd arrived in Prague.

That backup plan involved more risks than taking down the convoy, chief among them Werich's tight security in Prague, together with the city's large civilian population. Bolan hated the thought of collateral damage and hoped they could finish this job in the midnight hinterlands.

"You're still all right with this?" he asked Reynek. "The PCR, I mean?"

"They are no better than Lieutenant Meisel," Reynek said, watching the countryside unfold beyond his window. "Criminals. Some of them likely murderers. It's your restraint with them I do not understand."

"Call it a quirk," Bolan replied. "They're soldiers of the same side—or at least they were before they got tied up with Werich."

"You believe so?" Reynek asked him. "I suspect that some

police in every jurisdiction take the job to profit from it and commit crimes with impunity."

"I hope you're wrong," Bolan replied.

Maybe Reynek had a point, but Bolan couldn't break his private vow. He *wouldn't* break it, even to protect his life.

He hoped that both of them—and Werich's prisoners—could live with that.

WERICH TOOK THE NEWS of Berger's death with admirable calm, by her standards. She could not shoot the messenger, because the news came in from Miloš Týrlová by telephone. Nor did she smash her cell phone once he'd disconnected, though the urge was nearly overwhelming. Still, had anyone who knew Werich been present to observe her as she spoke, then closed her phone, they would have recognized her sizzling rage.

She had not harbored any great personal fondness for the middle-aged accountant, although he'd been competent enough in laundering her money through the years. And had enriched himself while doing so, of course. He had been a well-paid bookkeeper but did not rank as one of Werich's friends.

In fact, now that she thought of it, she had no friends per se.

Hundreds of people counted on her for their salaries, their bribes and benefits. Some were engaged to die for her, if need be—bodyguards and drivers pledged to take a bullet if it came to that—but none would do it out of love or admiration. Loyalty from subordinates was purchased, then maintained in equal measure by rewards and fear. As for the individuals with whom she dealt as equals, they enjoyed her services and benefited from covert association with her syndicate in other ways too numerous to catalog.

But none of them were *friends*.

All would forsake her in a heartbeat if she lost her wealth, her influence, her private army and her supply of nubile flesh ripe for the plundering. If she were *ordinary*, and they passed her on the street in Prague, not one would grace her with a second glance.

Which meant she had to hold the line, yield nothing to her

enemies in this or any other struggle for control. One crack in the facade could finish her, and she had taken hits aplenty, as it was, in recent days. In her imagination, she could see the first sharks circling, sniffing after blood. Hanns Lortzing from Düsseldorf would love to claim her territory, as would Pavol Rudnay from his base in Bratislava. Neither one would move against her when she was at full strength, but if Werich started losing ground...

It must not happen. She would hold fast to her hard-won empire of the flesh, regardless of the cost in blood and suffering. New soldiers could be found, eager replacements for the men she'd lost so far. And if the so-called statesmen she had bought and paid for thought they could desert her with impunity, they had a bitter lesson coming to them.

This was war. And Lida Werich was determined not to lose.

ANTONIN NAVRÁTIL CHECKED his watch to verify that they were still on time. There'd been a holdup leaving Nové Zámky, when a couple of the kids got sick from something they had eaten, but they'd made up time since then by cutting out the normal stop for use of lavatories at the journey's halfway point. What did Navrátil care if his unwilling passengers suffered discomfort on the trip to their new homes?

Before this time tomorrow, most of them would wish that they were back inside the trucks, driving forever without end, instead of servicing the scum that paid good money for the pleasure of their company.

Speaking of money, Navrátil would make six thousand euros for his time this evening, riding shotgun on the cargo culled from towns and villages across Slovakia, western Ukraine and southern Poland. Not a fortune, but it wasn't bad for sitting on his *prdel* in a truck and watching the dark countryside scroll past outside his window.

It was Navrátil's fifth trip for Werich, and so far he had not used the AK-47 or the pistol that he carried for security. None of the guards he supervised had fired a shot in anger yet, although there'd been an incident where one of them was drunk and started taking potshots at the moon. Navrátil had disarmed the fool, reported him to Werich's people, and the man was never seen again.

Simple.

The shipments were not interrupted, he supposed, because Werich or someone from her syndicate had bribed police on both sides of the border. This time, Navrátil had been advised, they'd actually have a PCR escort to Prague, joining them when they crossed the border from Slovakia. Some kind of turmoil in the capital, apparently, and Werich was not taking any chances with her merchandise.

In the beginning, Navrátil had thought about what he was doing, bearing kids and women to a life of pain and degradation far from home, but he had lost no sleep because of it. His father and his grandfather were criminals, the former shot down by police after a robbery in Liberec when Navrátil was only six years old. He'd grown up sly, mean and contemptuous of all authority, had been incarcerated as a juvenile and twice as an adult for crimes of violence. Why should it matter to him what became of total strangers, he thought, if his boss paid up on time?

The thought of being shadowed by police from Hodonín to Prague made Navrátil uneasy, but it was not his place to complain. Werich presumably had chosen officers who could be trusted not to interfere with business. One more reason Navrátil would never trust a *polda*. If the cops had any tricks in mind, however…

Navrátil had briefed his men on the peculiar circumstance of this night's convoy. Most of them had heard about the trouble back in Prague—vague rumors, wild surmises. No one knew the truth for sure, but Navrátil had warned each man to stay alert for any hint of danger.

Which included any shady moves by the police. If one or more of them was bent on double-crossing Werich, they would pay for it with blood. Of course, if Navrátil was forced to kill policemen Werich had dispatched to help him, he would have to seek more money.

Asking, not demanding, which could be a fatal error.

Meanwhile, he could sit back and enjoy the scenery—or lack of it, since the new moon illuminated next to nothing of the hilly Slovakian countryside. Next stop, the border crossing where he hoped the customs agents had been paid enough to pass the trucks along without demanding any kind of bonus for their trouble. You could never tell, of course, and Navrátil carried a roll of cash to make up any difference, just in case.

Damned greedy *zkurvysyni* ruined it for everyone.

"I'M STILL SURPRISED that Česká Televize went along with it," Reynek said.

"Think of the ratings," Bolan replied, half smiling in the Volvo's dashboard light.

"But what if someone at the station calls the PCR?"

He shrugged. "It makes no difference. We drop them two blocks from the spot where your guy has the cameras waiting, and we're gone. As far as who turns out to meet them, well, the more the merrier."

In fact, it was a relatively simple plan, assuming Reynek and Bolan were able to dispose of Werich's convoy guards. Pack all the prisoners into a single truck, with Reynek at the wheel, and trail Bolan's Volvo into Prague. Release them near the site where television cameras would be stationed, ready to record their stories—which would include a statement written by Reynek, naming Lida Werich as their kidnapper. Even if no one from the convoy actually read the document on camera, it would be picked up by the media and would unleash a storm of questions aimed at persons in authority.

"Some of them may not follow your directions," Reynek said. "What if we lose them at the drop point?"

"Then, at least they had a chance," Bolan answered. "Maybe they phone or send a message home from Prague, get reconnected to their families."

"And if those families don't want them back?"

Another shrug. "We can't reform the world," he said. "Just fight one battle at a time."

"If this works out, Werich will not be happy with tomorrow's morning news," Reynek observed.

"Least of her problems," the big American replied. "She's still got us to deal with, and she may not know that Murton's on his way back to the States."

"So many problems all at once." Reynek could not suppress a smile.

"It's why she gets the big bucks," Bolan suggested.

"Big koruny," Reynek said, correcting him.

"Whatever. If we pull this off, she'll wish she'd picked another business."

"And if we don't?" Reynek asked.

"Well, then, it's been good to know you."

"It's funny, if you think about it."

"Ha-ha funny," Bolan inquired, "or funny strange?"

"A bit of both, I think," Reynek answered. "I've spent my whole adult life trying to uphold the law and have nothing to show for it. Now I'm an outlaw and a fugitive, but I feel better than I ever have before."

"I wouldn't recommend it as a rule," Bolan said, "but I appreciate your help."

"Don't thank me," Reynek said. "I do it for myself and for the victims. When I think of all the wasted years…"

"Not wasted. I'm betting you've helped someone every day that you were on the job."

Reynek wondered if he was going maudlin in what might turn out to be the final hours of his life. "Not help enough," he said. "And not the people who were most in need. If I had been like you from the beginning—"

"Then you wouldn't be a cop," Bolan said. "You might not even be alive."

"I could have dealt with Lida Werich at our first encounter."

"And she would have been replaced by someone else within a day," Bolan said. "No victory is permanent. The fight goes on."

"It's just as well that you're a soldier," Reynek said. "Your skill as a motivational speaker is *hovno*."

It was the first time Bolan had laughed in Reynek's presence, and he kept it up for nearly half a mile.

LIEUTENANT GUSTOV MAHLER was not pleased with his assignment. Captain Karel Turek, in approaching him, had tried to skirt the subject with a lot of double-talk about "security" and the "integrity of borders," but he was not fooling Mahler. This would be a risky, miserable job that left him feeling as if he could shower for a week and still feel dirty.

Mahler, unknown to the captain, had taken security precautions of his own. While the officers selected for his team were suiting up and drawing weapons from the armory at headquarters, he'd written out a near-verbatim transcript of his conversation with the captain from the PCR's Agency for Particular Activities of Criminal Police, signed it and dropped it in the station's outbound mail, addressed to an attorney friend he knew from classes at the Czech Technical University in Prague.

Whether it would result in any action being taken, if he died on this night, was anybody's guess. At least, if there was any consciousness beyond the grave, Mahler would know that he had tried.

Meanwhile, the filthy job.

Guarding civilian vehicles in transit from Slovakia to Prague meant either drugs or human trafficking. And since two trucks would mean the largest shipment of cocaine or heroin in Eastern European history, Mahler was betting that the cargo would be women bound for brothels in the capital.

Or, worse yet, children.

Mahler had grown accustomed to corruption in his nine years with the PCR, but stubborn optimism prompted him to hope that each new incident would be the worst he had to face. Each time that he was proved wrong, Mahler moved the bar and hoped his fellow officers would try to salvage some vestige of dignity before they plunged headlong into the sewer occupied by the animals they were expected to arrest.

He'd thought of quitting, but in recent years the country's unemployment rate had ranged from eight to ten percent, and what else was he suited for? To give up his comparatively decent salary and benefits to walk the streets in search of work, while a wife and twins waited at home hungry, was not an option Mahler cared to contemplate.

At least, if I get killed this night, he thought, *they have the life insurance.*

He was seriously angry by the time they reached Jihlava, seventy-odd miles southeast of Prague and roughly halfway to their destination on the border. Mahler wished that he could turn around or radio to headquarters, tell Captain Turek to come out and babysit the gangsters and their contraband himself. It would have cost his job, of course, but he'd have gone out on a high note, as a legend to the honest officers still seething in the ranks and hoping for a chance to carry out their duties properly.

Too late for me, Mahler thought, perfectly disgusted with himself. *Whatever happens next, I'm in the soup.*

And he could feel it coming to a boil.

15

"Looks like the spot," Bolan said.

"Yes," Reynek agreed. "They must pass by here from the border checkpoint."

They were well ahead of time, 11:25 p.m., with ample opportunity to choose their fields of fire and settle in. They'd left the Volvo a mile back, concealed from view of passing drivers on a narrow, unpaved road that seemed to go nowhere. The hike up to their present site through darkness had consumed sufficient time for whispered planning in the dark, before a scouting jog to eye the border crossing with its pair of lazy-looking guards.

"Figure the customs men have had the heads-up, and they'll get their payoff when the trucks arrive," Bolan surmised. "Let's hope they stay out of the way when it gets hairy."

"They aren't paid to fight," Reynek said. "From the look of those two, I suspect they'll run halfway to Trenčín when the shooting starts."

"Suits me," Bolan replied. And then, the sore point. "If the PCR is sending out an escort, they should be here anytime."

"Believe me when I say they mean no more to me than any other criminals," Reynek said.

"We'll still go with the bullhorn first," Bolan said. "If they want to change their minds and split, so much the better."

"Don't expect it," Reynek cautioned. "With the mind-set I've become accustomed to, they follow orders without question. Tell them to arrest a man, they do not ask the reason. Tell them to ignore another, they pretend he is invisible."

"You're doing what you can," Bolan replied. "Breaking the mold."

He had his hardware laid out, ready for engagement when the targets showed themselves. The Vz. 58V rifle gave him autofire, with backup from the Dragunov if Bolan needed a precision shot. The URG-86 frag grenades would be a last resort, their shrapnel uncontrollable within its calculated kill zone. If it came down to his ALFA pistol or the trench knife on his belt, Bolan supposed they would be out of luck.

"Someone is coming," Reynek said, head cocked to listen, turning to the west.

Two engines, by the sound of it. They waited, cloaked in darkness, while twin pairs of headlights bathed the road in front of them and twenty feet below their chosen vantage point. First in view was a standard Škoda Octavia prowl car with seating for four. Behind it, a Volkswagen T-5 Transporter brought up the rear, potentially carrying eight to ten officers.

Trouble.

If both cars were packed, cops might outnumber Werich's goons. He didn't want to think about that—not until he had to, anyway.

And it would not be long.

Antonin Navrátil saw the PCR vehicles waiting as his truck rolled past the border checkpoint, leaving two obese and well-paid customs agents in its wake. The second truck proceeded without stopping, also covered by the bribes he had delivered to the two fat fools. From that point on, it ought to be smooth sailing with their escort into Prague for the delivery of their new merchandise.

"Stop here," Navrátil told his driver, when they'd put the border stop a hundred yards behind them. Both men had seen the PCR lieutenant step out of his Škoda, one hand raised to flag them down, and Navrátil was happy to cooperate.

The officer reached up to grab the truck's side mirror, stepped onto its running board and rose to face Navrátil at eye level. "Let's be clear," he said in an unfriendly tone. "I don't know what you're carrying, and it should stay that way, for both our sakes. You have an escort into Prague, and that is all. We leave you at the address I was given, and we're gone. *Dohodnuto?*"

"Yes, that's agreed," Navrátil said.

He wasn't sure what had upset the officer, nor did he care. Each member of the team was paid to do a certain job; no more, no less. Navrátil didn't give a damn what the lieutenant thought of him or his employer. Make that *their* employer, since they both were eating out of Werich's finely manicured hand.

The cop returned to his vehicle—was it possible to walk with angry strides?—and got it turned around. The PCR van followed, then Navrátil's truck fell into line, the third link in a four-vehicle caravan. It was a warm night, good for driving with the windows down, a fresh breeze bringing Navrátil the scents of country living that he never smelled in Prague. Wood smoke, fresh-turned earth and growing things.

He was relaxing when the voice boomed out at him—or, rather, at the two police vehicles out in front of him. It seemed to come from everywhere and nowhere, all at once.

"You officers! Remember who you are! Why are you working with these thugs and murderers? Leave now, and you may still survive! You officers..."

The whole thing started over from the top again. Navrátil saw the Škoda stop, then the Volkswagen van behind it. In the lead car, necks were craning, the policemen trying to discover where the eerie voice was coming from—and then a gunshot echoed in the darkness. Suddenly, Navrátil's shirt was drenched with the blood and mangled tissue from his driver's shattered face.

REYNEK WAS HALFWAY through his second warning to the PCR detachment and repeating it verbatim when the crack of Bolan's rifle stung his ears. Downrange, he saw the driver of the lead truck jerk, then topple over sideways in his seat, the man beside him scrambling to unload that leaky burden and avoid the next incoming shot.

Reynek finished his cautionary spiel, rushing the final bit, then set down the bullhorn and picked up his submachine gun. The police car and its trailing van edged forward fifteen, maybe twenty feet as Bolan shot the man behind the wheel of Lida Werich's second truck, then doors flew open and the occupants spilled out.

Damn it!

Reynek had time to count an even ten of them before they started firing toward the bluff that he and Bolan had chosen for their sniper's perch. With just a twinge of sadness, he selected one man from the pack and fired a three-round burst into his chest. The officer—a younger man than Reynek, frightened-looking—tumbled over backward and lay still.

Then it was chaos, gunmen leaping from the cabs and rear decks of the two trucks, firing blindly into darkness, emulating the police as they sought cover on the north side of their vehicles. Bolan's automatic rifle stuttered, dropping one of them, and then another, neither burst striking the trucks themselves. Reynek heard screaming from one of the trucks, a girl's or woman's voice—then, sickening him where he lay, a wail that sounded like an infant's cry.

He swung back toward the PCR men huddled under cover of their vehicles, stitching holes along the left side of the Škoda and the larger van.

Whatever kinship he had ever felt for fellow officers was swept away by Reynek's fury, seeing these in service to the worst scum of the earth. Whatever feelings he had previously classed as hatred or contempt paled into insignificance beside the rage that presently consumed him. If he had been in uniform, Reynek would instantly have stripped it off and gone to battle naked, rather than behind a badge of shame.

Reynek wished he had a rocket launcher, settled for a stun grenade instead and lobbed it overhand in the direction of the two police vehicles. It exploded in midair, some ten or fifteen feet above his adversaries' heads, lacking the force to render them unconscious in the open, but still loud enough to shock them.

One forgot himself, rolled out from cover to escape the flash and noise, perhaps believing it had been a frag grenade. Reynek was ready, pumped three rounds into the dazzled target's skull and watched his form go slack.

"Pojd' ven a bojovat," he muttered to himself. "Come out and fight."

BOLAN HAD COUNTED TWO MEN jumping from the tailgate of each truck below him, two more in each cab. With three down, that left three still fit for combat—and he knew there might be others lurking in the rear compartments, covering the hostages. He couldn't use grenades or strafe the cargo bays to drive them out, which meant that he would have to take the fight up close and personal.

He nudged Jan Reynek, caught his eye and said, "Try warning off the cops once more."

"They wouldn't listen," Reynek countered.

"Even so, it helps distract them," Bolan said. "I'm going in."

A grimace creased the sergeant's face before he said, "Be careful, eh?"

As if.

There were degrees of caution, moving into danger on the battlefront, but none of them would qualify as being careful. Bolan ducked back from the precipice above his enemies, stood up and jogged due east to reach a point behind the two trucks, where the bluff sloped down to nearly match the level of the highway. Pausing there, he checked both ways along the road and found the guards for Werich's convoy firing toward the point where Reynek's voice echoed from the bullhorn once again.

To Bolan's right, as he had hoped, there was no sign of either skittish customs officer.

He broke from cover, leaped across a roadside ditch with standing water at the bottom and began his run across two lanes of open asphalt. Halfway through it, someone shouted from the second truck, and Bolan saw a muzzle-flash above its tailgate aimed his way. He hit the deck, rolled twice and held his fire for fear of striking hostages inside the truck.

Cowards. With human shields at hand, they weren't about to show themselves if it could be avoided. Bolan's task: to root them out regardless and eliminate the threat, once and for all.

More rounds incoming. Bolan rolled again, then half rose, lunging toward a weed-choked ditch that lay along the north side of the highway. Splashing down, he wondered for a heartbeat whether there were any vipers in the Czech Republic, then dismissed the thought and focused on the human predators before him.

One heaved into view as Bolan raised his eyes above the roadbed. He was short and squat, advancing in a crouch that further minimized his height. Bolan fired once into the center of his body, striking him somewhere below the belt buckle, and saw him drop.

How many left to go?

The Executioner could only count them as they fell.

OVER THE CRACKLING SOUNDS of gunfire that surrounded him, Lieutenant Gustov Mahler heard the bullhorn's amplified voice speak again. "You officers! Why are you dying to protect the scum of Prague whom you should be arresting? Throw down your weapons! Leave now, and those of you who still remain may leave in peace!"

Mahler was torn, despite the fact that he had seen two of his men shot down. They truly had no business here—unless it was, as their opponent said, to jail the traffickers whom other traitors to the PCR had called upon them to protect. Their midnight mission had perverted everything he understood about the law and civilized society. It fell light-years beyond the simple act of taking money to ignore a traffic violation or to let a dealer peddle drugs to willing users.

They were aiding slavers in the delivery of helpless victims to a fate that Mahler thought was worse than death.

"Enough!" he shouted to the officers around him. "Cease fire, all of you!"

One of them rounded on him, almost snarling. "Cease fire? They've killed Rudolf and Václav."

"No," Mahler replied. "*I've* killed them. If I hadn't followed orders from a pig who's sold his soul, we wouldn't be here now. They'd both still be alive."

"What are you saying?" another asked.

Mahler felt them watching him, made eye contact with each of those who still remained huddled behind the cars. "We have a choice," he said. "First, we can trust the men who've ambushed us and try to leave, unarmed."

An angry murmuring among his officers reflected their displeasure with that option.

"Or," he told them, "we can do the job we should have done here in the first place. Grab whatever bastards from the trucks are still alive and take their victims back to Prague. Find someone in the government to help them get back home."

"We can't just walk *out there*," one of the frightened cops reminded him.

"What have we got to lose?" Mahler replied. And rising to his full height, he moved around the rear end of the van.

He eyed the bluff, no winking muzzle-flashes up there at the moment, then turned toward the closer of the slaver's trucks. Raising his pistol, he advanced, shouting, "Lay down your weapons. You are all under arrest for human trafficking!"

The first thug Mahler met gaped at him for an instant, heard the order repeated, then smiled and raised his automatic weapon. Mahler shot him in the face and bellowed at the officers still crouched behind the van.

"Come on, you *zbabělci!* It's never too late to do the right thing!"

WHEN BOLAN SPLASHED into the roadside ditch, he'd figured that the shooter from the truck would follow him. And sure enough, just as he raised his head to check the road, a burly gunman dressed in black dropped from the tailgate to the pavement, landed awkwardly, but caught himself before he fell and managed to stay upright.

The guard swiveled toward Bolan, tracking with some model of Kalashnikov, its outline unmistakable. He fired a burst without seeming to aim, then waddled toward the ditch. Bolan rolled backward in the water, waited for the round moon-face to show itself, then triggered three quick rounds that blew away the upper half of it, punching the dead man back and out of sight.

Soaked through and dripping, Bolan rose first to his knees, then to a crouch. He peered up at the tailgate of the nearest truck, where other faces anxiously returned his gaze. Female, as far as he could tell, age indeterminate. Assuming that he couldn't comfort them in English, Bolan let it go and crawled back onto blacktop, searching for the other convoy guards.

But as he passed the tailgate where the frightened captives hovered, Bolan realized that something odd was happening. Behind the trucks and the police cars, angry voices shouted back and forth at one another. Someone giving orders, someone else plainly refusing them. When hectic gunfire suddenly erupted, Bolan hit the deck and rolled under the truck, using its bulk for temporary cover.

He saw the rest of it in fragment images, legs for the most part, dashing back and forth. Some were in uniform, the rest in ordinary slacks or jeans. Above the legs, men traded point-blank shots, some crumpling to the asphalt, others reeling back in search of cover, too late to find it. Spent brass clattered on the roadway. Gun smoke reeked, competing with the sharp metallic scent of blood.

As best Bolan could tell, there'd been some kind of falling-out between the cops and Werich's soldiers. That was fine with him, if it reduced the hostile odds, but Bolan wasn't jumping in the middle of it, with police lives on the line. Better to wait it out, he thought, and see what happened next.

Look for an exit from the killing ground that didn't put him in a body bag.

He was about to creep out on the driver's side and hope that no one noticed him before he sprinted into darkness, when the shooting stopped. Too late to move? A strained voice called out something, and another moment passed before he heard Reynek answer through the bullhorn, speaking Czech. The colloquy went back and forth for several rounds, before the sergeant switched to English.

"Cooper! It's safe! Come out!"

Trusting Reynek was right, Bolan slid out of cover and stood up.

REYNEK DID THE TALKING, pausing to interpret portions of the conversation as he went along. The leader of the skittish PCR detachment was a slim lieutenant in his thirties, showing signs of shock but still in charge. The others were a mixed bag, understandably suspicious, far from trustworthy in Bolan's view.

But it was Reynek's show. Somehow, he'd managed to convince the cops who still remained alive to switch sides in the middle of the fight. They'd finished off the guards employed by Werich, and it appeared that all the captives—thirty-two of them, ranging in age from early twenties down to five or six years old—had managed to survive the fight unscathed.

Reynek stepped close to Bolan, lowering his voice, although it seemed that none of the policemen ranged before them was an English speaker. "The lieutenant, Mahler is his name, says that his men will drive the trucks into Prague and find someone to care for this lot. He's not sure if that would be the Ministry of Justice or Labor and Social Affairs. He'll make sure they're protected and settled."

"You trust him?" Bolan asked.

Reynek shrugged. "He helped us here. He also says that he will call the media before they get to Prague so nothing can go wrong. No getting lost or sidetracked and forgotten in the bowels of the bureaucracy. I've let him know that I will check on it and visit him if he reneges."

"All we can do, I guess," Bolan agreed, "under the circumstances."

"Yes."

"What's waiting for these guys when they get back to Prague?"

"Perhaps an inquiry," Reynek suggested. "The lieutenant

thinks his captain may wish to avoid embarrassment, if possible."

"The captain's name?"

"I have it," Reynek said. "It's time that he retired."

"So, we just walk away? They're good with that?" Bolan asked.

"They are relieved that *they* can walk away," Reynek replied.

"Let's go, then," Bolan said.

Hiking back to reach the hidden Volvo, they were quiet for the first half of their trek, then Bolan said, "We still need to find Lida Werich."

"I have an idea on that," Reynek said.

"Oh?"

"Perhaps the captain who she called to organize this guard detail knows how to contact her."

"You think?"

Starlight revealed no warmth in Reynek's smile.

"I think I need to ask him," he replied.

16

Bolan was pleased with the location that Lieutenant Mahler had selected for his statement to the media: Prague's Old Town Square, bustling with tourists who had no idea they were about to watch a group of total strangers making history.

The television cameras were in place before the army-surplus trucks arrived, unloading weary officers with a bedraggled group of young women and children. Bolan and Reynek watched it from across the square, overshadowed by the Gothic Church of Our Lady before Týn, Reynek translating Mahler's words as they were wafted to him from a bank of amplifiers.

"He is sticking with the script as we agreed," Reynek said. "An anonymous tip sent them to the border, where they intercepted a slaver's convoy… Two officers and seven gunmen from the trucks were killed… He's sketching in the circumstances now… Women abducted from their native towns and villages… Some of the children sold by parents through a false ruse of adoption in the West… And yes, he just named Lida Werich as the suspected ringleader. That's finished him, I think."

"You never know," Bolan replied. "She doesn't strike me as the kind who'd file a slander charge, much less show up in court."

"She doesn't have to sue him," Reynek said. "Mahler just killed his own career. He'll be assigned to shit work from now on, until he logs enough complaints from his superiors to be dismissed. Werich may wait that long to kill him, but she isn't known for patience."

"He won't have to deal with Werich if we find her first," Bolan said.

"Still the same old problem, eh?" Frowning, Reynek said, "But I may have the solution."

"Oh?"

"The captain Mahler named last night."

"So, what about him?" Bolan asked.

"He takes his orders straight from Werich, or at least her second in command. I think he should know where to find her."

"And you're planning on asking him?"

"Why not?"

"Well, if you ever planned on going back to your career…"

"That's finished now, like Mahler's," Reynek said. "Maybe we'll buy a bakery together. Sell *kolache* to the real police."

"You *are* the real police."

"Not anymore. But I can still do this one thing," Reynek said. "I can talk to Captain Karel Turek."

WERICH FELT AS IF her head would burst and spray her brains across the room. The images in front of her on television, the policeman's droning voice, had spiked her blood pressure into the stratosphere. She hurled a glass of vodka at the TV screen and missed, cursing her own ineptitude in language fit to blister paint. As liquor dribbled down the screen, the police officer went on and on.

Using her name.

"Do prdele! Mrdat! Piča! Seru na tvoji matku!"

She was running out of swearwords, seethed at the deficiency, straining to invent new insults for the weary-looking man who stood before the world, fingering her as a pimp, a defiler of children. The fact that all of it was true did nothing to placate her.

Werich wished the men she'd sent to drive and guard the trucks were still alive and standing in her office at that moment. She would happily—yes, *joyfully*—have killed them all again. Using an ax, perhaps, or a machete. Take the leader of the team outside, douse him with gasoline and light him up where he would not rain ashes on her carpet.

Given some time, she would destroy the loose-lipped PCR lieutenant and his family. Three generations back should be enough to satisfy her. She would massacre the other members of his team, their loved ones, friends, acquaintances. Before they died screaming, she would make sure they knew exactly why they had descended into hell.

And what about the man who'd chosen them to serve her?

Captain Karel Turek.

Didn't he deserve a personal reward for his pathetic—no, *disastrous*—choice of officers to safeguard this most vital shipment?

Yes, indeed, she thought.

She could invite him to a private meeting—cautiously, aware that she'd be under scrutiny until things normalized in Prague—then spring the trap, torture him for a week or two, then make him disappear forever. The alternative: send soldiers she could trust, if any such existed, for a blitz attack that made the captain an example of what happened to officials who betrayed her.

Either way, she meant to see him dead and find a more reliable successor at the PCR.

For when this storm died down, as moral outrage always did, and the city returned to business as usual, Werich meant to be there, in the midst of it, grabbing her share of the money hand over fist.

REYNEK HAD REFUSED to let the big American join him when he confronted Captain Turek, knowing the man would balk at taking lethal action against a police officer under any circumstances. Having crossed that line himself, from which there was no turning back, Reynek let Bolan record his phone call to the captain, threatening to blow the whistle on Turek's connection to the Werich syndicate unless he met Reynek alone, outside the Church of St. Castulus in the Jewish Quarter.

Reynek knew that it could be a trap, and so he went prepared, his submachine gun tucked into a canvas shopping bag slung over his right shoulder, hand inside the bag, clutching around its pistol grip. On a cord around his neck, his cell phone dangled with its camera turned on, broadcasting images and sounds in real time to the spot where Bolan sat waiting in his Volvo half a mile away.

Whatever happened next, there'd be a record of it. Turek's trap, if trap it proved to be, would close around him, too.

As he approached the church, Reynek saw Turek standing out in front, hands in the pockets of a gray trench coat. He looked like someone from an old spy movie, waiting to hand off a roll of microfilm before the KGB swooped in to make arrests, and Reynek realized that they had passed each other in the hallways of the Ministry of Justice more than once. Slowing, the sergeant scanned the neighborhood as best he could, searching for watchers, but found none.

"I am alone," Turek said, as if reading Reynek's mind. "And you?"

"Just as you see me," Reynek said.

"I've been looking for you," Turek told him. "Now, we meet at last."

"Too late to help you," Reynek answered.

"Is it?"

"I could ask you many things."

"About the choices I have made? Alliances with Lida and the others?" Turek shrugged. "It's money," he told Reynek. "Nothing more."

And that's the end of your career, Reynek thought. As he said, "In fact, however, I have only one question."

"Ask it, by all means."

"Where can I find your partner?"

"Lida?" Turek smiled. "Oh, you've found her to be, shall we say, elusive?"

"But no longer," Reynek said. "Her life for yours."

"It's come to that, then? Very well." The captain gave him an address on Na Příkopě, between Old Town and New Town, in the heart of Prague. "At least, that's where she had her nest two days ago. You may have smoked her out by now. If so, I cannot help you."

Reynek repeated the address for Bolan's ears, then told Turek, "I'll be back to see you, if the information's faulty."

"I doubt that," the captain answered as the right-hand pocket of his trench coat suddenly exploded. And again.

The bullets staggered Reynek, ripping through his chest. His knees buckled, colliding with the pavement, but he still had time to empty half the submachine gun's magazine before he toppled forward, pleased to see the Parabellum rounds make Captain Turek dance. A moment later, Reynek was facedown on the sidewalk, watching as his blood streamed toward the larger pool of Turek's and began to form a crimson lake.

BOLAN HAD REACHED the shooting site five minutes after gunfire crackled from his cell phone, but a motorcycle cop was there ahead of him, examining the lifeless bodies, making sure no one among the first wave of pedestrians walked off with any of the guns involved. Bolan drove past, swallowed the sense of loss he felt and checked the voice-activated tape recorder that lay beside his cell phone on the Volvo's shotgun seat.

The tape had captured all of it.

He memorized the Na Příkopě Street address and navigated toward it, while he popped out the recorder's small cassette and put it in his pocket. When he had the time to spare, he'd mail it to the major television station there in Prague—what Reynek had called Česká Televize—and let them run with it, if they decided it was newsworthy.

By that time, Bolan's work in the Czech capital would be complete.

Or he'd be dead.

But if it went that way, he wouldn't be alone.

Na Příkopě Street—literally "On the Moat"—was a posh boulevard lined with banks, shops and cafés, connecting Wenceslas Square with the Square of the Republic. The address

Reynek had obtained from Captain Turek had a bank on the ground floor, with several floors of offices above and a penthouse apartment overlooking commerce on the street below. Across the street, the rooftop of a tall building gave the Executioner a clear view of the penthouse and the bustling Na Příkopě traffic.

It was nearly perfect.

Nearly, since the penthouse windows had been coated with reflective film that gave its tenant total privacy. Whoever lived within could stare outside all day and night without being seen. Good for the tenant; lousy for a sniper.

Bolan had to flush her out.

He dialed the number that had linked him to his target once before and told the man who answered, "Put her on."

Adjusting to the English, Werich's bodyguard replied, "Who's this?"

"I met her trucks last night," Bolan replied. "She may have seen it on the news."

The phone thumped down, was silent for the better part of half a minute, before Werich's voice came on the line. "You've been a busy little bastard, eh?"

"And I'm not finished yet," he said.

"Oh, no?"

"The captain gave you up before he died."

"Am I supposed to know what that means?" Werich asked.

"His name was Turek. Big man with the PCR, from what I understand. He likely would have kept his mouth shut if he'd known a tape was rolling."

"Do prdele!"

"I'm afraid I didn't catch that," Bolan told her.

"Why should I believe you?"

"Don't. Sit back and wait until you see it on TV. I'm betting that the talking heads will eat it up after the press conference this morning."

"Am I supposed to beg for mercy now?"

"It wouldn't matter," Bolan said. "But what I'm hoping is that you'll stay put and wait for the police to smoke you out."

"And where do you suppose I am?" she challenged him.

He rattled off the address, heard the phone slam down again and lost the link.

Smiling, Bolan returned the cell phone to his pocket and picked up the Dragunov.

WERICH RAGED through the penthouse apartment, shouting at her lackeys, shoving some of those she passed who were not moving fast enough to suit her, cursing intermittently as she snatched small items and dropped them into the maw of an oversize handbag.

"I told you to *hurry!*" she bellowed. "What part of that can't your small brains understand? *Seru na tvoji matky!* You move like old women who've just been sedated. Get cracking, *zatraceně!*"

Passing Miloš Týrlová in the central hallway, she clutched his arm, her fingernails like talons, causing him to wince involuntarily. "The car," she said, "is it downstairs?"

"Ready and waiting, ma'am."

"That's it, then." Turning from her captain to the flat at large, she shouted through its spacious rooms, "We're leaving *now!* Anyone who lags behind is fired! Anyone one comes with me but doesn't bring the items I assigned to him is dead! *Move out!*"

Týrlová was at her side when Werich reached the private elevator, used her key and watched the door hiss open. Half expecting gunmen to be waiting for her in the elevator car, she'd reached inside her bag to grip the pistol hidden there, but no one threatened her.

She stepped into the car with Týrlová, half a dozen others crowding in behind them. Werich made no effort to count heads or see what they were carrying. She'd meant exactly what she said before she left the flat. Failure was not forgiven nor forgotten in her world.

But what was left of that world, with the exposure she'd received? The losses she had suffered? What was there to salvage from the ruins? Could she hold her own against the vultures who'd be circling already, eager for a chance to pick her bones?

Perhaps.

But only if she managed to survive the next few hours and remain at liberty.

The elevator always made her stomach tingle as it raced down to street level. She'd enjoyed that feeling in the past, a private little thrill. But not on this day. Already queasy from her gross public humiliation, Werich had no appetite for any more surprises. All she wanted was to escape, lie low until she could regroup, mount her defense, and then—

The elevator door opened again. Týrlová led her across the building's lobby, past the marble entrance to the ground-floor bank, her party trailing as they reached the street. Outside, in unrelenting daylight, Werich squinted at the glare and ducked her head, running to reach her limousine.

IT WAS AN EASY SHOT from Bolan's vantage point, but still he didn't take it lightly. It had been a while since he had pulled the trigger on a female adversary. It went against the Bolan grain, a lesson taught from infancy.

You don't hurt girls.

But Werich hurt girls every day. She had consigned an untold number to the living hell of sexual slavery, from which the sole escape was death. Not only girls, but *children,* some of them mere infants, as he'd seen himself at last night's convoy stop. And if she lived, the list of victims would keep growing, countless lives destroyed, her prey condemned to a fate literally worse than murder.

So, he took the shot.

The stadiametric rangefinder built into Bolan's telescopic sight gave him the range. Its reticle permitted him to mark the target as she ducked to clear the open back door of her waiting car. The Dragunov bucked once against his shoulder, and he saw the blond hair part downrange, erupting into crimson mist.

The rest was a matter of mopping up. Five shots to drop Werich's companions where they stood in stunned confusion, gaping at her corpse. Two tried to run, one turning toward the building he'd just left, the other breaking to his right. Neither was fast enough. Bolan considered taking out the limo's driver as he stumbled out to view the carnage, but decided that he'd done enough.

At least, for the here and present.

Epilogue

Deputy Minister of Justice Vladimir Neff felt relaxed as his ca[r] rolled through New Town en route to pick up the guest he'd in[vited] to lunch. Despite an undeniable sensation of uneasiness h[e] had experienced throughout the morning, following the new[s] on television, Neff currently felt as if a crushing weight ha[d] been lifted off his shoulders, permitting him to move again.

Permitting him to smile.

The first news had been terrible: the convoy intercepted[,] victims and police parading for the TV cameras and dropping names. Of course, they didn't know *he* was involved, but ther[e] was still the threat that Werich would make good on her per[sistent threat to telling all she knew to anyone who'd listen, i[f] and when she ever went to court in Prague.

Well, problem solved.

The bulletin announcing Werich's death had been a shoc[k] to Neff, though he had always been aware of certain dangers i[n] her chosen trade—and all the more so during recent days. H[e] didn't know who'd pulled the trigger, and he didn't care. Ideally, Werich's death would go down in the records as anothe[r] unsolved crime related to whatever they were calling syndi[cated criminals these days.

He'd scheduled lunch to celebrate and to update Jakub Grossmann on their near miss with disaster. Grossmann had alread[y] heard the news, of course, though he was wisely reticent t[o] speak about it on the telephone. Over their lunch at Kampa Park beside the river, they could hash out the details in privacy and

Neff could reassure the judge that all was well. No one need ever know of their involvement with the Werich syndicate, since the crazy *fena* and her captain from the PCR were dead and gone.

Blood washed away their problems, after all.

Grossmann was waiting for him on the street outside the courthouse on Hlavni Mesto. He ducked into the limousine and seemed relieved to be there, barely touching the hand that Neff offered to him. They rode in silence to the restaurant and let the stunning hostess lead them to their table on the riverside. Only when they were settled there, with wine in front of them, did Grossmann speak.

"I've been concerned," he said. "You understand, I'm sure."

"There is no longer any need," Neff said.

"Because *she's* been removed?" Grossmann inquired.

"That, and the captain," Neff replied. "Between the two of them, the secret dies."

Grossmann sipped wine and frowned. "She paid so many others, as you know."

"Each one of them concerned about himself today," Neff said. "Who would be fool enough to open that Pandora's box with a confession? Nothing good could come of it."

"Perhaps, with all that's happened—all that's been exposed—one may feel conscience stricken."

"Then, I think, a priest would be involved," Neff speculated, "not the prosecutor's office or the media."

"I hope you're right."

"Your Honor, you may rest assured of it."

"In that case," Grossmann said, "I feel my appetite returning." Picking up his menu, he asked Neff, "What seems the best to you this afternoon?"

Neff was considering his options when he heard a kind of popping sound, as if someone had struck a melon with a cleaver, and something resembling tomato sauce with meat spattered his menu, gobbets of it flying past to stain his shirt. Neff blinked, then raised his eyes in time to see the judge collapsing sideways in his chair, fully a quarter of his skull missing.

Instinctively, he glanced off to his left, toward the Vltava, where a smallish motorboat carrying two men stood halfway out from shore. One of its occupants was kneeling, turned in profile toward the restaurant, and...*aiming* something?

Neff made the connection, tried to lunge back from the table, but the movement was too little and too late. In the split second that remained to him of consciousness and life, he reckoned that he saw the bullet coming, growing larger until it was everything, filling his world. He barely felt the impact as it cored his skull, and he was dead before the first scream from his young, attractive waitress wafted toward the river, swallowed by an engine's growl that quickly faded out of range.

* * * * *